Mabel & the Cat's Meow

Prequel to *Mabel Gets the Ax,*
Book One in the *Mysteries of Medicine Spring*
cozy mystery series.

Mabel & the Cat's Meow

Prequel to *Mabel Gets the Ax*,
Book One in the *Mysteries of Medicine Spring*
cozy mystery series.

Susan Kimmel Wright

ISBN: 978-1-7373459-0-9

Interior editing and design by:
Sue A. Fairchild, sueafairchild74@gmail.com

Cover photo from © Nynke Van Holten | Dreamstime.com

For more information on this book and the author visit:
susankimmelwright.com

Dedication

For the cats I've shared my life with, who've already used up all nine lives and pit-patted on to the next great adventure: Tiger, Puss, Duke, Diana, Sammy, Rufus, Peter, Paw Paw, twins Chester & BeeGee, Cappy, Sydney and Ferris.

You've each left your pawprints on my heart.

Chapter One

The sound puzzled Mabel. She'd been walking down Ash Street, basking in the afternoon sunshine filtering through the overhanging maple trees and breathing the aroma of fresh-cut grass. The lazy little town of Medicine Spring was a welcome break. She'd been lucky to be able to spend her annual two-week vacation—plus one day, due to the upcoming July 4th holiday—here with Grandma, who was recuperating from a hip replacement.

Up till now, the growl of the lawnmower, which a shirtless middle-aged man pushed around his yard behind a trim boxwood hedge, was all she'd heard. That, plus the chirps and warbles of a few birds in the branches. Mabel was glad to get away from the noises of downtown Pittsburgh, where she'd been a lowly backroom associate attorney ever since her law school graduation twenty years ago.

When she heard the out-of-place noise again, she stopped, straining to place what it was. Maybe a whimper?

The mower passed close to the corner where Mabel stood, and for a moment, that was all she heard. Even the birdsong directly overhead was swallowed up in the roar. The man waved and grinned. Sweat streaked his face beneath a red bandana, seemingly chosen to complement the patriotic bunting across his porch overhang.

He turned the front corner then retreated, cutting a swath toward the back patch of grass separating his house from its neighbor, another Victorian with a porch awash in yellow gingerbread moldings. The sturdy growl of the mower faded a bit.

Now, Mabel heard the cry again. Her heart jolted. It sounded like a baby.

Okay, she told herself, turning in a slow circle where she stood. Someone around here has a baby. Pretty soon they'll stick a bottle in its mouth or change its diaper, and everything will be fine.

Still Mabel hesitated. She knew exactly nothing about babies, but if the baby needed something, wouldn't it be screaming? That's what they always did in movies and TV shows while clumsy adults blundered around in a panic. This whimper she'd heard sounded small and weak. Even to her inexperienced ears, the cry seemed to suggest real frailty.

She looked uncertainly at the yellow-trimmed Victorian as the cry came again. The house looked uninhabited. But surely the sound was coming from there?

The mower advanced on her once more. "Excuse me!" Mabel waved her arm. "Does your neighbor have a baby?"

The man winked and sucked in his belly roll. "Nice day, isn't it?" he yelled back.

As he turned the corner again, Mabel frowned. He appeared to think she was flirting with him. Sure, she was in her mid-forties ... okay, maybe late forties ... but he was clearly way too old for her. Clearly ...

She backed a few tentative steps toward the neighboring house. Yep, definitely unoccupied. In fact, all the lower windows appeared to be boarded over.

Mabel started to turn away, but that little cry came again. Her stomach tightened.

A breath of breeze lifted the maple leaves that shadowed her spot of sidewalk, carrying the scent of someone's backyard grill. Mabel eyed the far porch corner. Were all the lower windows boarded? Was there an opening somewhere a wandering toddler could've crawled through? *Or—the* thought chilled her— *abandoned a baby?*

The mower sounds had stopped by now, and there was no sign of Mower Man.

Just take a minute and check, she told herself. Her feet had already started moving toward the steps of the wraparound porch.

The floorboards, painted a low-gloss gray, a shade darker than the house clapboards, seemed solid under her weight. The street was empty of cars and no other pedestrians were out in the heat. Still, something made Mabel cast a furtive look around her as she crept along the porch toward the back of the house.

She jumped as a goldfinch burst from a snowball bush just below the railing next to her. The bird flew a few feet away to another bush, from which point he launched angry scolding even she could understand.

"Sorry," she mumbled. "I won't bother your nest."

Mabel reached the end of the porch. Another, skinny set of steps led down to a narrow, unpaved driveway running between the house and side yard. They visibly tilted right, perhaps due to settlement. Feeling a bit akilter, Mabel clutched the railing as she descended.

She followed the driveway, seeing only boarded windows at her level, plus a leprechaun door—less than two feet square—set low in the house wall. The rusty metal was ornately scrawled with the word Majestic. *Coal chute.* Grandma's house had one too.

Mabel looked up. The second-floor windows all appeared intact, but she heard the cry again, sounding clearer from her new position.

All the way around to the rear of the house she went, staring at nothing more than boarded-over first-floor windows, a padlocked back door, and one tiny basement window that still had glass in it.

She looked up again. A noticeable crack ran from a small hole in the corner of the pane over the back porch roof. All the other second-floor windows appeared secure and had been left unboarded. One window at the far right, though, looked open a crack at one end, as if it had become jammed in a cockeyed position. It offered possibilities.

If she could get up there somehow, she'd be able to put her mind at ease. She couldn't risk leaving a baby in distress.

Her conscience balked. *You can't just go willy-nilly into somebody else's house.*

It's obviously an empty house, she argued with herself. *Nancy Drew would definitely do it. Trixie Belden would not even hesitate.*

Bolstered by the example of her childhood heroes, Mabel studied the situation. A ladder would be ideal at this point. Mabel glanced around her wishfully, but nothing appeared. Not that a woman of her somewhat generous proportions ought to be clambering up an untested ladder, anyway.

A plaintive cry drifted from the open window. Briefly, Mabel considered seeking assistance from the neighbor with the mower. But he didn't seem to be outside anymore. And she didn't want him to think she was trying to strike up an acquaintance.

Mabel contemplated her sturdy walking shoes with the rubber-tread soles. She could do this. She just needed a safe approach.

A rickety-looking fire escape was mounted below the jammed window. It didn't reach the ground because, she imagined, you were supposed to lower it the rest of the way when you climbed out of your window during a fire. Studying it, Mabel considered jumping.

Even if she could miraculously grab hold, her muscles weren't up to hoisting her bulk aboard, American Gladiator style. All she could count on — if she actually reached it, which she wouldn't — would be rusty scrapes and scratches on her hands, and a trip to the ER for a tetanus shot.

Trying to ignore the cries from overhead … were they growing weaker? … she focused on a shed perched in the back fence corner. It would be locked too, of course, but she should at least try.

Mabel jogged across the yard, sweat beading on her forehead. To her amazement, as she lifted the latch, the door swung open on well-oiled hinges. Unsurprisingly, it was empty except for several old license plates nailed to the back wall, and a coiled garden hose. And a ladder.

The aluminum step ladder was light enough to carry and appeared well built. Mabel couldn't quite lift it off the ground and balance it, but she managed to drag it with relative ease. To her delight, it reached within a couple feet of the bottom of the fire escape.

The climb to the fire escape seemed easy in comparison to her scramble onto the platform, which shook in an unsettling manner. Mabel felt the seam of her camp shirt sleeve rip, as she stretched to grab on. A moment later, her shorts snagged on a random bolt as well.

Sweating more from stress than exertion, Mabel sank gratefully onto the open floor grate, panting, and inspected the hole in her pants. *Darn it.* She loved these roomy cadet-blue shorts, airy with a touch of spandex. The big V-shaped rip sat right in the seat where even Grandma's wizardry with a needle would never inconspicuously close it.

She might have grieved her ruined shorts a moment longer if she hadn't heard the tiny cry once more from the opening above her head. Grunting, she pulled herself to her feet and climbed the few steps to the windowsill.

Mabel struggled to lift the sash, but the wooden frame seemed to have swollen. That was likely why it hadn't been latched. Whoever had attempted to close the window had probably jammed it down as far as it would go and then just decided to leave it that way till they could get back to fix it. It was summertime, the house was empty, and this was a second-floor window, after all.

Sweat trickled into her eyes as she pushed and shoved. She raised a hand to wipe it away, but just in time, caught a glimpse of the dust clinging to her damp fingers.

It occurred to her she was in an awkward position were someone to see her up here. She needed to get inside before that could happen. Mabel hit the sash frame with her fist, hoping to loosen it. Then, she shoved again with all her might.

The window moved upward half an inch. Surprised and encouraged, she repeated the process until the window stood open far enough for her to attempt to squeeze through. She had never wished more she were a size eight.

Cautiously, she swung a leg through the opening. So far, so good. Mabel flattened her torso and sucked in her breath, thrusting herself into the open space.

Except she didn't quite make it all the way through. She couldn't move forward and couldn't move back. She was stuck.

Sweating in earnest now, she pushed forward again. And then her shirt caught on a splintered section of wood.

Saying a quick prayer for deliverance, Mabel stopped trying to shove her way through. Instead, she thrust her back upward against the sash. This time, it rose another inch, and she struggled through to the other side.

Mabel landed face down on the bare, dusty floor. Breathing hard, she pushed herself onto her feet. Her arms and legs shook, but she'd made it.

The noises had escalated and seemed to be coming from inside this room. She stilled and listened again. Maybe the sound wasn't a baby after all. Maybe just a bird?

Mabel looked around, but there was no one else there, and not even a stick of furniture. A putrid smell hung in the air, suggesting an expired mouse somewhere on the premises. Mabel prayed it wasn't a rat or a rabid raccoon.

Cat? The sounds were almost too delicate to be a cat. Still, she was no longer certain the cry was quite human either.

A closed door in the corner beckoned her closer. Holding her breath, Mabel tugged at the handle. Seemingly swollen, it too held fast for a moment before suddenly giving way and toppling Mabel backward.

As she staggered, trying to stay on her feet, a small blur of black-and-gold fur shot from the closet and streaked toward the open window. The blur resolved itself into a skinny, half-grown tortoiseshell kitty and crashed into Mabel, who'd wobbled sideways in an attempt to regain her balance.

The cat whirled and raced toward the hallway with Mabel following, trying to move deliberately so she wouldn't further terrify the frightened animal.

"Here, kitty," she called. "It's okay. I won't hurt you."

Mabel's heart still chugged in her ears, but her breathing had slowed now that she knew only this little kitty was up here. She crossed to the open room across the hall, hoping the cat hadn't run downstairs instead or up toward the attic.

She crossed the threshold just in time to hear a faint tinkle of breaking glass as the tip of the little cat's tail disappeared out the broken window she'd noticed from below. Mabel caught hold of the door frame, the cat forgotten. A silent scream lodged in her throat. This room wasn't empty.

Chapter Two

For a sickening moment, the room seemed to spin as Mabel clutched the door frame and swallowed hard. The foul smell of death now hit her full force.

Her brain registered only fleeting impressions. A few gold-colored candy wrappers on the floor. The buzzing of flies. The faint hum of the neighbor's lawnmower once again making its back-and-forth circuits of the yard next door.

A shape on the dusty floor. A body lying on its back. The body of a *human* male, dressed—incongruously for this heat—in khaki slacks and a quarter-zip-style navy sweater. His face a pulpy-looking mass …

Mabel might have screamed, but maybe that was only in her head. Without a moment's hesitation, she scrambled for the open window, squeezed herself through onto the fire escape, and clambered down the ladder. She trembled violently, shaking the ladder.

She stepped down too soon, missing the last rung of the ladder and scraping her shin as she landed. Her ankle turned just enough sideways to hurt. She limped toward the street, still screaming in her head.

Mabel reached the shimmering heat of the blessed sidewalk, gasping at the clean, cut-grass-scented air. She kept running, stumbling on her aching ankle.

The lawnmower abruptly shut off. "You all right?" the man called after her as he made his way to the sidewalk.

Two houses away, the family with the grill looked up. Their toddler in the wading pool stopped splashing and stared at her.

"Miss?" Mower Man panted, still jogging after her.

Mabel swung around, sucking air. She couldn't speak.

He caught her arm and looked her in the eyes. "What's wrong? Why are you screaming?"

Sheepishly, Mabel realized her silent screams had at some point moved from her mind to her mouth. Out of the corner of her eye, she saw the mother gather her now-crying toddler and an older boy and drag them inside the house while dad came over to investigate.

"I ..." Mabel struggled to control her ragged breathing. "There's ..." Should she start with the body? Or why she had just climbed inside a house that didn't belong to her?

A pair of power walkers approached from the other direction. With a confused rush of relief and embarrassment, Mabel recognized Grandma's best friends, Miss Birdie and Ms. Katherine Ann.

The two ladies, both well over eighty and seemingly unaffected by the heat, broke into a jog when they caught her eye. "Mabel, baby," Miss Birdie called. "What on earth?"

Miss Birdie's sharp, dark eyes looked Mabel over, and she tsked and pulled her into her wiry arms. Mabel towered over the diminutive, brown-skinned woman, but shamelessly let herself be comforted. Ms. Katherine Ann, an improbable, vivid redhead, uncapped and handed Mabel her water bottle. She wore a jogging outfit in a turquoise version of Miss Birdie's magenta, a couple sizes larger to fit her sturdy frame.

As Mabel gratefully gulped water, Ms. Katherine Ann scowled and fingered her pepper spray. "Did some low-life try to grab you, dear?" Both old ladies seemed to scan the bushes for perpetrators before casting suspicious glares over the two hovering men.

The dad, still carrying his barbecue spatula, backed up a few paces.

"No, no ..." Mabel swallowed and straightened up. "Police. We need the police. There's been a ..."

Her audience's eyebrows rose.

Murder? Was it murder? Or just some incredible, face-smashing accident in an empty room?

Mabel frowned. "There's a b—a dead body." She pointed. "Back there."

"She's overheated," Ms. Katherine Ann said. "She needs to sit down."

The dad hurried to open the gate in his hedge.

Miss Birdie shepherded Mabel, firmly gripping her arm. "Are you sure, baby?" Her voice conveyed doubt.

"Yes!" Mabel said, a bit wildly, pulling her arm away. Immediately, she felt ashamed. "I'm sorry, ma'am. I'm kind of ... agitated."

Calmly, Miss Birdie recaptured her arm and led her through the gate. "I know, baby. I'm sure we all would be, too, in your place."

"There's a dead man," Mabel said, "In that house back there."

She saw the glances the group exchanged as she settled into the mesh seat of a lawn chair on the dad's deck. Behind him, a drapery twitched—probably the mom watching from a safe distance.

"Slow down." Mower Man clutched her arm. "Say what?"

As quickly as possible, Mabel told her story, with many interruptions to explain about the noises, how she'd climbed up, and about the cat. The men exchanged eye contact and got to their feet. "You ladies stay here," the dad said. "Let me just let my wife know what's happening."

When he disappeared inside, Mower Man began pacing back and forth across the deck. His lips moved, but he wasn't saying anything Mabel could hear. He'd been sweaty when he grabbed her arm, but now she could see it trickling along his neck and chest.

The dad reemerged, stuffing a cell phone into his shorts pocket and carrying a baseball bat. "You ready?"

Mower Man sucked in his shirtless gut and gave a curt nod.

"You just wait here, okay?" the dad said to Mabel. "We may need you."

She nodded. "I believe we'll stay right here with her, young man," Miss Birdie told him, and Ms. Katherine Ann squeezed Mabel's hand. Mabel felt a wave of gratitude.

As the two men crossed the lawn toward the street, their voices drifted back. "You better let me do the climbing," the dad said.

"I'm not over the hill yet," Mower Man told him. "No need for climbing, anyway. I got the keys."

As they waited, the mom reappeared carrying a jug of water and three glasses on a tray. A fat toddler boy in a soaking wet playsuit clung to the cuff of her shorts. She introduced her family—Amanda, Carlo, and Buster Diodato.

Though the woman looked askance at Mabel, she kindly poured water and asked if she needed anything.

"I'm okay," Mabel said, though her stomach roiled. To her relief, the two old ladies stepped in and engaged the mom in conversation, smiling at her little boy's antics, while Mabel took cool sips of water and watched the street.

After a seemingly interminable time, the dad reappeared, redder and sweatier than when he'd left.

As he made his way back across the lawn, Mabel stood up. He nodded at them, his mouth tight.

"Dead, all right." He leaned heavily against the deck railing.

Miss Birdie pulled a red Jitterbug cell phone from her pocket and flipped it open. The numbers on the call screen were enormous. "I'm calling 911."

"Already did," the dad puffed. "They ought to be here any minute. Pete stayed to guard the scene and let them in. I'm going to go back over. Sorry, honey. Don't know how long this is gonna take." He looked at his wife. "Can you finish grilling?"

"I'll come with you," Mabel said. "They're going to want to talk to me anyway."

"We should be going too," Ms. Katherine Ann rose to join Miss Birdie, who already stood at the railing.

"Thanks so much, dear," Miss Birdie called back as the two old friends slowly descended the steps.

Mabel had assumed they'd continue on their way, but to her surprise, the women trailed after her and the dad. Carlo, she reminded herself. And he'd called the other man — the mower — Pete.

The police had already rolled up silently and parked at the curb next to the boarded-up house, emergency lights flashing. A paunchy, dark-skinned policeman, sweating in what appeared to be a polyester-blend uniform, introduced himself as Sergeant McAllister and his partner as Officer Yang. His damp scalp glistened through close-cropped, wiry curls.

McAllister pulled out an old-fashioned pad and began making notes as Mabel described finding the body and explained once again what had motivated her to climb inside the old house. McAllister called for back-up.

"Which of you's Diodato?" McAllister grunted.

The dad raised his hand.

"You got the key, right?"

"Um, no." He pointed. "Mr. Dombroski has it."

"Let's go," McAllister said. "You stay here a moment, Miss. Okay?"

Mabel felt a combination of relief and disappointment. Now that the initial shock and horror had faded a degree, she sort of wanted to take a calmer look around … just in case there was a clue she'd missed. "I—"

An impatient hand gesture from the sergeant stopped her in her tracks.

"Okay."

The four men disappeared inside the front door of the house. Mabel sighed.

The old ladies craned for a better look, but so far, there was nothing really to see with the bottom windows blocked and no sign of movement behind the dark squares of unlit second-floor panes. Mabel, still a bit sick from the shock of finding the body, struggled to quell her anxiety. How much trouble would she find herself in as a result of her well-intentioned trespass?

Chapter Three

Miss Birdie had been watching Mabel clumsily pace the sidewalk on her tender ankle while the police went to look at the body, but on one pass she reached out and touched Mabel's arm. "What did that man look like, baby? Been trying to figure if Katherine and I might know him. Tell us again."

Mabel swatted away a buzzing fly that landed briefly on her cheek. She swallowed hard, remembering the flies swarming around the man on the floor.

"I'm sorry, baby. If it bothers you too much, I don't want you upset."

"No. It's okay. He, uh, wasn't in the best shape. But he was short." She closed her eyes, trying to focus on basic details the heat and flies hadn't altered. "Maybe my height or so."

"Five-nine or so?" Ms. Katherine Ann asked.

"Shorter," Mabel said. "I think. I'm five-nine, and he looked shorter to me. He was White ... and maybe thirty-five or forty? His eyes were open, but ..." Her voice trailed off and she swallowed again. "I couldn't make out much of his features."

Ms. Katherine Ann touched Mabel's arm. "We understand."

A second cruiser had pulled in behind the first and the two officers went inside the building. Soon, a paramedic ambulance arrived, silent but flashing its lights. An EMT stepped out of the passenger side, talking on his radio.

More people, undoubtedly curious about the emergency vehicles, had started gathering. A twenty-something couple with two leashed spaniel pups came to a stop. One of the dogs promptly sniffed the front hedge

17

and squatted. Three teenage boys tipped their bikes and stood watching the house. Here came another old lady in lilac capris, a red tank top, and huge dark glasses. She was shaped like a butternut squash, and her hair sat atop her head like an oversized dandelion puff.

She hailed Grandma's friends as she limped toward them. "What's going on?" she yelled from half a block away.

Miss Birdie and Ms. Katherine Ann exchanged a despairing glance.

Miss Birdie cleared her throat as the woman drew near. "This is Mabel's granddaughter, little Mabel. She's been helping her after the hip job. Baby, your grandma's and our friend, Thelma Neuhaus."

After the initial introduction, Mabel tuned out the threesome as best she could, partly out of courtesy and partly fear she'd be asked to recount her story again. She wandered a few steps away, alternating between watching the growing crowd and watching the house, as the paramedics headed inside.

Cars had now pulled over and some people had gotten out to rubberneck. Mabel wandered a bit farther from the crime scene while keeping an eye out in case the police beckoned her. As she stood at the fringes of the crowd, a man tapped her shoulder.

Mabel yelped and spun around.

The skinny, tousle-headed man, perhaps in his late thirties or early forties, stuffed his phone into a jeans pocket. "Sorry. Didn't mean to startle you."

"It's okay. I'm a tad on edge."

"What's going on over here?" He tipped his head toward the house.

Mabel hesitated. He didn't look like a reporter, but these days, who could tell? And she hadn't been expressly told to keep her mouth shut.

"I … they found a body," she said. That fact would soon be clear enough when they wheeled it out.

Mabel heard a soft gasp behind her and realized others had not only heard her but were milling closer, like a curious herd of cows around a picnicker in their pasture. "Really?" the man who surely wasn't a reporter said, seeming oblivious to the encroaching eavesdroppers. "Any idea who?"

What appeared to be a bunch of county crime scene techs was entering the building at that moment. Of more immediate interest to Mabel — not to mention concern — was a woman in businesslike khakis and a summer-weight light-blue blazer exiting a nearby car with what appeared to be a handheld voice recorder.

"Excuse me." Mabel cast a semi-apologetic look at her questioner and elbowed her way through the crowd. When she looked back, Mabel's questioner had also apparently removed himself from the reporter's path and was now standing at the far fringes, scrolling his phone.

The reporter had stepped a few yards from her vehicle and was speaking with a man who was waving his arm at the house and speaking animatedly as the herd of onlookers crowded around them.

***

The sun was riding a bit lower in the sky by the time Mabel returned to Grandma's street. She'd managed to elude the reporter's microphone but had still been forced to wait for an officer to come out and take her statement. She was thankful he'd moved her to the house's wraparound porch for the interview, away from all the inquisitive ears.

While describing the actual discovery of the body, Mabel had felt on solid ground. The facts were pretty straightforward. She'd squirmed, though, over the questions about why she'd entered the house. Her motivation, though it had seemed compelling at the time, now sounded unconvincing, even to her.

"You thought you heard a … baby?" He'd raised an eyebrow, pen poised above the notepad.

Mabel had nodded. "Yes, sir."

"But it turned out to be a cat?"

By the time he'd flipped the pad back into his breast pocket, she'd been sweating profusely from discomfort as much as the humidity. She'd make a lousy criminal, she decided.

Mabel wiped her forehead and daydreamed about a frosty lemonade.

Grandma's house sat at the quiet dead end of Carteret Street, only a single block long, and the street ran right up to a short section of rail fence, behind which a wooded stretch of township park sprawled over several acres. Three houses sat to the right, two on the left, all on big lots.

The house anchoring the left corner where Mabel turned was the Sauer mansion, a reservedly elegant example of American Arts and Crafts style. The house, once owned by the Sauer family, was best known as the site of a grisly 1939 double ax murder but now occupied by the Medicine Spring Historical Society.

She scurried past the brooding relic, which admittedly creeped her out. Just as she passed the front steps, a bicycle bell shrieked directly at her back. Mabel jumped sideways, stumbling over the old carriage block by the curb, heart skipping, and barely stayed on her feet.

She clutched her chest and whirled around.

The bicyclist, Helen Thornwald, nimbly hopped off her robin-egg blue bike and set the kickstand with barely a smirk for Mabel, let alone any apology. The elderly pillar of the historical society smoothed down a long navy skirt and tucked in her ruffled white blouse, then locked her bike to the old cast-iron hitching post.

The look Helen gave her seemed calculated to suggest that securing the bike had been for Mabel's benefit. As Grandma's contemporary, backyard neighbor, and longtime nemesis, she always treated Mabel as guilty by association. Of what, Mabel certainly couldn't say.

With a curt nod, Helen headed up the broad front stairs clutching an oversize key ring. Not for the first time, Mabel pondered Helen's uncanny resemblance to Miss Gulch in the Wizard of Oz. In every way.

Mabel passed the overgrown vacant lot separating the Sauer House and Grandma's. The deep, two-acre field belonged to Grandma, but was mostly occupied by wildlife. When she reached the Victorian farmhouse, she entered the kitchen by the side door.

Grandma's big, shaggy cattle dog mix, Barnacle, jumped on her and danced around her feet until she put him out on his backyard run. His coat looked gray at a distance, but was actually peppered black-and-white. For reasons unclear to Mabel, cattle-dog people called that blue.

Mabel made a beeline for the fridge. "I'm home!" she called over the sound of one of Grandma's afternoon shows.

Grandma didn't answer—possibly because she didn't hear Mabel, or just as possibly, she was letting Mabel know she was trying to follow her show. Mabel poured herself a lemonade and took a long, thirsty swallow. So good. She wiped her brow again.

Mabel topped up her glass and headed to the living room. "Hi, Grandma. Can I get you something too?"

Grandma shook her head, eyes still glued to *A Stolen Life*. "Have a seat, baby."

She mumbled daily about her doctor's orders not to use her ancient recliner while her hip healed because the footrest could only be lowered by pushing her legs down. Still, Grandma obediently sat bolt upright in a kitchen chair, dressed in a short-sleeved cotton housecoat and sturdy shoes with Velcro straps. She had one hand on the TV remote, which rested on an end table next to a half-cup of coffee, and the other on the prepaid cellphone Mabel had forced on her for the duration. Her thick mop of chestnut hair, so much like Mabel's, was streaked with gray and standing pretty much straight up.

Mabel set her glass on the cluttered coffee table and collapsed onto the couch, now crowded in next to the rented hospital bed Grandma was using during her convalescence. She'd texted Grandma she'd be late but was chafing to tell her what had delayed her. Grandma knew most of the older folks, at least, in Medicine Spring, and maybe she knew the people who used to live in the house now occupied by only a skinny cat and a dead body.

Chapter Four

Grandma muted the final commercial. "Lemonade looks good. Would you mind fetching me one?"

"That's why I'm here." Mabel hopped up and went to the kitchen. She let Barnacle back indoors. He immediately headed to his water dish and drank with much noisy splashing while Mabel filled another glass with lemonade.

Mabel wondered if Grandma had even heard her earlier when she'd offered to bring her a drink. Probably not. When Grandma got lost in the continuing saga of Emily, Cliff, and the other trouble-prone denizens of Meadowvale, she might as well be in a trance.

When the show ended, Grandma smiled at Mabel. "Hot out there?"

Mabel pulled her sticky shirt out from her body. "Yeah. If you remind me, I'll water the garden after supper."

"What kept you, baby? Thought you'd be back way in time for the show."

"There was an incident. It'll probably be on the news later."

Grandma had a habit of leaving the TV on even when she wasn't watching. She knew she was wasting electricity, but said it was like company whenever she was alone. Unfortunately, the habit had become so ingrained she often left it on even when somebody else was in the room, making conversation difficult. At the mention of police, the remote clicked to "off."

"Mabel? What on earth are you talking about the police?"

Mabel shoved at Barnacle, who'd parked himself on the couch with his steamy body weight resting companionably against her. She launched into her story, but immediately needed to explain again what she was doing in somebody else's house.

"Mabel Josephine Browne, why on earth would you do that? Not to mention you could have fallen to your death. Or a broken leg."

Grandma's own name was also Mabel Josephine Browne, and Mabel sometimes thought Grandma just liked saying it.

After Mabel had told the whole story, including how she'd happened to run into Grandma's friends on the sidewalk, Grandma shook her head. "Wish I'd been there." She slapped her right knee. "If it wasn't for this darn leg, I'd've been right there with the girls."

"I know you would." Mabel quirked her mouth in sympathy. "But hey, if you hadn't had hip surgery, I wouldn't have been here to find the body in the first place."

"I suppose you're right." Grandma looked not the least bit mollified.

"In a way, you're the whole reason the body ever came to light."

That thought seemed to cheer her somewhat. "What did the guy look like? The one you found."

Mabel described him as she had for Miss Birdie and Ms. Katherine Ann. "Too young." Grandma shook her head again. "Doesn't sound like Phil Gundersen. No good reason for him to be in there anyway."

Mabel raised her eyebrows.

"Guy who lived there till last spring. They're in Arizona now."

"Did they just retire or what?"

"I guess so. Never really knew them. They didn't go to our church, and your dad and them were way ahead of Gundersen in school."

Grandma shifted in her seat. "I wonder now …" She squinted her eyes shut. "Trying to think if I heard of anybody else leave town or go missing. There was a younger woman … you sure this was a man?"

"A hundred percent."

"Doggone. The girls and I will have to put our heads together on this," Grandma said as if accepting a job assignment.

She picked up her phone but didn't dial right away. "Might not even be local. We got more people just passing through these days, going too fast, trespassing all over the place. Now they're even getting themselves killed in other people's houses. Would you mind taking Barnacle out for a bit, baby? He needs a walk."

Hearing his name, Barnacle popped up, focusing a slobbery grin first on Grandma and then on Mabel.

"Sure." Inwardly, Mabel rolled her eyes. She loved Barnacle, but he was tireless. When he didn't get enough exercise, he turned his energies to his other hobbies. These primarily consisted of digging holes in the back yard and gnawing the most prized possessions in the house, such as Mabel's new sandals and Grandma's treasured childhood baby doll.

"Just take him out in the field and throw the ball. That's what I've been doing since my hip went bad on me."

Mabel changed into jeans and sneakers, then held her breath while she sprayed herself with insect repellent.

Between poison ivy and the mosquitoes around the low areas, the field was far from appealing this time of year.

Correctly reading the signs, Barnacle leapt at her and whined at the door. His white-tipped plume of tail waved eagerly. He whirled in circles and barked, then darted into the small utility room off the kitchen which held the washer-dryer and a basket with his toys. He returned with a well-chewed tennis ball, which trailed the last strands of its fuzzy covering and a garland of drool.

Soon, Mabel would have to touch that thing.

For the next half hour, Mabel threw the ball as far into the weeds as she could, hoping Barnacle would have to search for a while. Invariably, he bounded back far too soon while Mabel attempted to carry on a phone conversation with her best friend Lisa.

"Lucky you!" For a petite kindergarten teacher, Lisa's obsession with true crime was disconcerting.

When Mabel didn't respond, Lisa rushed to explain. "Of course, it was horrible for you. I know that. And obviously for the guy that got killed. Horrible," she repeated. "But I mean, somebody had to find him, right? And you got to do that. It's sort of a once-in-a-lifetime thing, right?"

"I certainly hope so."

Lisa snorted. "You're too much. Hey, are you going to be on the news?"

"Nope. I managed to dodge the TV news teams. But for sure the discovery of the body ought to be on."

"Oh, hey! My cake timer just went off. I better run."

"You want to come over for dinner? Grandma's really getting bored. She'd love the company."

"Good deal. Give me about an hour, okay?"

Mabel, as always, was done playing ball before Barnacle was ready to call it quits. Seeming to sense what she had in mind, he hung back, holding his slimy treasure in his mouth as he stared back at her.

"Look, Barnacle." Mabel tempted him with a treat from her pocket. He shifted his feet restlessly and more drool dripped from his jaws.

When his appetite finally got the best of him, Mabel exchanged the treat for his precious ball. After he was done gobbling his dog biscuit, Barnacle resumed jumping at Mabel as she headed back to the house.

Mabel threw the ball again, hard, then wiped the slime from her fingers. She congratulated herself on her brilliance in throwing the ball toward the back yard.

Unfortunately, Barnacle saw through her ploy and immediately ran back out to the field with his mangled toy. It took another ten minutes of wrangling to get him on the leash and back inside.

Lisa arrived promptly at six dressed in a buttercup-yellow tank top, white shorts, and sandals, her sleek black bob freshly clipped. How could she look so cool? Mabel lifted her own heavy mass of chestnut waves up off her neck. She wistfully contemplated getting a short, summer cut, but her fear of looking like a bowling pin won out.

"Come on in." She felt around in her pockets for a hair tie. "We're having sliced ham and Grandma's potato salad."

"I thought you were taking care of her," Lisa whispered.

"She hardly lets me do anything. Says it's good for her to get up and do things." Mabel rolled her eyes. If she kept doing this, her eyes were going to roll on down the road like the Gingerbread Man. "Says I work too hard and I need my vacation."

Lisa giggled. "It's what keeps her young and feisty." She made her way into the living room with a bouquet of daylilies.

Dinner conversation was lively. Afterward, Grandma predictably shooed them onto the porch saying she'd "just wash these few dishes in no time." With that, she turned her back and started running water into the sink as she stood there with her walker.

As Mabel and Lisa sprawled themselves onto the porch swing, Lisa said, "I can't help feeling guilty, seeing her washing our dishes. Just exactly what *have* you been doing the past few days?"

"Well, I'm here in case of falls. And there are things she really can't do, like getting into that claw-foot bathtub, so I heat water for her to take a sponge bath. Stuff like that."

Lisa grinned. "Okay, Nurse Mabel."

Mabel started to defend herself, but then grinned back and shrugged. "It's actually been pretty easy. I do worry about her falling, but so far, so good. And it's the first summer vacation I've had since I was a kid."

"Did your Grandma have any idea who your body was?"

"Nope. Who'd be in a boarded-up house like that? I think if they find the owners, the cops will soon figure it out, though."

"Didn't you say the neighbor has a key too?"

"Well, yeah. I guess they'll be looking at him too."

Mabel shook her head, as the image of the victim rose in her mind again. "I'll never forget that face. It was awful. I'm going to see it in my sleep."

Lisa patted her knee. "Hey, tell me about your cat."

Mabel frowned. "I hope she's all right. She ran like she was okay, I guess, but she was way too skinny. Who knows how long she was stuck in that hot closet with nothing to eat or drink?"

"Well, she's free now, thanks to you."

"I wonder if she belongs to someone ..."

They talked for about a half hour, idly swinging and enjoying the bit of evening breeze stirring the trees. A wasp seemed to be building a nest above the front steps. Mabel would have to check if Grandma had any spray. Somewhere nearby, a wood thrush poured liquid notes onto the air.

"Mabel!" Grandma's yell made Mabel scramble off the swing, making it lurch wildly and bang off the wall.

Lisa followed as she rushed back inside. "Your body's on the TV."

Chapter Five

Grandma stood in the living room doorway, one hand on her walker and holding the remote in the other as she turned the sound up. Mabel felt the speakers vibrate her teeth.

"Look, there's Mabel!" Grandma pointed the remote at Mabel being interrogated by the police on the murder house porch.

"Here, better sit down." Mabel ushered her to her seat.

The reporter, a perky brunette, recounted the discovery, periodically gesturing and nodding at the house. "According to others on the scene, an intruder got more than she bargained for when she broke into the house earlier today."

Mabel shot up from the couch. "Intruder!"

She glowered as Lisa shushed her. It wasn't as if people two blocks away couldn't hear Grandma's TV as clearly as if they were in the same room.

"Hey, look." Mabel's righteous anger faded. "It's my cat."

As they watched, the little tortoiseshell slipped around the corner of the house, headed toward the back. "There *is* something wrong with her hind leg."

"Aw, poor thing. You need to do something."

Grandma waved her hand for them to quiet down, and vainly attempted to turn the speakers past 100.

Obediently, Mabel and Lisa buttoned their lips, though Mabel knew the segment would be available on the station's website later.

The reporter stuck her microphone under a tall, bushy-haired man's nose. Mabel squinted — that must be the guy who'd talked to her.

The young man threw his hands up and backed away. Undeterred, the reporter turned to Miss Birdie and Ms. Katherine Ann's plump friend, Thelma, while a few of the younger people in the crowd popped up behind her, waving and mugging for the camera.

"Hey!" Now Grandma was the one talking. She waved a hand back and forth. "Oh — that one! What's the name?"

"The woman being interviewed?"

Again, the hand flew back and forth. "No. That's Thelma Neuhaus. No one wants her opinion, but she'll give it to you anyway." She pointed. "That guy. The one who didn't want to talk."

Mabel's ears perked up. "With the wild hair? He talked to me. Do you know him?"

Grandma heaved a big sigh and sank back into her seat. She didn't reply, and Mabel didn't press. More and more, Grandma had trouble remembering things, and it made her very frustrated.

Lisa caught Mabel's eye. Mabel shrugged.

Mabel's phone vibrated in her pocket. She groaned and quickly sent it to voicemail when she read the caller ID. Mom must've just watched the same newscast, and she was already calling to interrogate her.

When the segment ended, the program shifted to the local debate over stream bank protection, and Grandma muted it. "It can't be who I first thought. He'd be way older. Can't remember the name anyway."

"Maybe if you and Miss Birdie and Ms. Katherine Ann put your heads together, it'll come to you," Mabel suggested. "You can look up the report online, or maybe one of them already saw it and recognized him."

"I hope so. My brain doesn't work right anymore." Grandma picked up her folded newspaper and ballpoint pen. "Could you turn on the floor lamp, baby? I need to finish my puzzle."

As Grandma's cell rang, Mabel tossed her head, gesturing to Lisa it was time to run for the door. She did not want to hang around for her mother's inevitable lecture about climbing into houses and finding murder victims, especially on Grandma's time.

Leaving Grandma with the phone tucked under her chin and supplied with her evening decaf and the tissue box, Mabel and Lisa headed out to search for the cat. Barnacle followed them to the kitchen door, his eyes sorrowful.

"Sorry, buddy, you wouldn't be helpful on a cat rescue mission," Lisa told him. "Poor guy."

"He'll live." Mabel adjusted the blue-and-orange fanny pack Grandma had forced on her. Inside was a high-powered flashlight and a slice of ham wrapped in foil — cat bait.

The evening had cooled somewhat, and smudgy clouds were massing in the west.

"You think it'll rain?"

"Supposed to, but I doubt it. They've been predicting rain for a couple days already, and zip." If it did rain, Mabel hoped it would wait till they were back at Grandma's.

As she and Lisa passed the murder house — the *ax murder* house, she corrected herself, since now there were apparently two murder houses in Medicine Spring — Mabel crossed the street.

"I can't believe you still do that."

"Only when it gets near dusk. Anyway, we're headed this direction."

When they reached the Victorian, the crowd had departed, leaving a few cigarette butts and candy wrappers on the pavement, and a section of battered hedge where someone had lost his balance when crowding too close.

Using a piece of tissue, Lisa picked up an empty soft-drink cup, a few of the scattered gold-foil wrappers, and a crumpled chip bag. "People disgust me sometimes."

"Where you going to put those?"

Lisa scowled and set them back down. "Do you have any hand sanitizer?"

"Of course." Mabel unzipped the fanny pack, a souvenir of Kennywood amusement park. "Whatever problems Grandma has remembering things, she still knows what to put in an emergency fanny pack."

As she rubbed her hands, Lisa scanned the house and most of the visible yard, now wrapped in yellow police tape. "I hope you find kitty, but if she's running scared, I doubt you'll be able to catch her."

Mabel sighed. "She's probably back inside by now, anyway, and that's off limits at this point."

"As if it wasn't before," Lisa mumbled.

Mabel gave her a halfhearted dirty look. "I know, okay? But she might still be out here somewhere if that hind leg's too bad for her to climb back up. She probably cut it going out a broken window."

"Well, what's the plan?"

"I guess just poke around a bit and see if she might be hiding in the bushes or something. Then if we spot her, try just sitting quietly with ham on our lap for a while."

Lisa curled her lip. "Sounds gross, but okay. Anything for kitty."

Mabel pulled out the Maglite. It was hardly bigger than her hand, but as soon as she turned it on an intense light beam shot across the yard. "Whoa."

"Check under here first," Lisa suggested, nodding toward the latticed crawl space under the porch. "We got a raccoon family under ours one summer."

Obediently, Mabel swung the light around, momentarily blinding Lisa. "Oops, sorry." She bent down and aimed the light beneath the porch. Because of the tape, she couldn't get very close, but the Maglite illuminated the space.

"Nothing. Darn it."

With Lisa at her heels, Mabel began a slow clockwise circuit of the edge of the yard, flashing the light through the bushes. "I don't want to stampede her," Mabel said.

"Here, kitty, kitty," Lisa called in her soft, gentle, kindergarten-teacher voice.

"Maybe it's better to be quiet."

"It probably doesn't make any difference. If she's hurt and scared, just the sight of us might make her take cover."

Shadows already blanketed much of the back yard, but Lisa paused at the looming bulk of the fire escape. "I can't believe you climbed up there," she whispered.

"Neither can I."

They turned the back corner toward the street.

Seconds later, a furious baritone boomed from across the hedges. "Hey, you — hands up!"

Chapter Six

Lisa screeched as both her hands shot up. Mabel's heart lurched and she dropped the flashlight. It still beamed through the grass where it landed. "Don't shoot!" she squeaked.

"Stay where you are." The voice was moving now, and soon Mabel saw a figure emerge through the bushes separating the house from the one next door.

Mabel recognized Mower Man, now wearing a shirt — the guy with the key to the house, who'd let the cops inside. He wasn't holding a gun. Mabel relaxed and lowered her hands.

"Just what do you two murder aficionados think you're doing? This is a crime scene."

Mabel glowered, partly shaken and embarrassed, and partly furious. "I'm well aware it's a crime scene." She retrieved the Maglite, flashed it in his eyes, apologized, and redirected it at a courteous spot near his left shoulder. "I found the body."

The man squinted at her face. "Oh, sure, I remember. You also broke in the place. What are you doing back here? This is off limits."

Still trying to control her shaking, Mabel drew a deep breath. She pointed, the Maglite sweeping in a bumpy arc over the house. "*That's* off limits. The yellow tape ends right there."

"You giving tours or what?"

"I don't appreciate your tone." Lisa peered around Mabel. "Who put you in charge, anyway?"

"As a matter of fact, the Gundersens put me in charge. The people who own this place. It's my job to keep an eye on it. Especially after what happened."

"You mean all the vandalism? Or people breaking in and getting murdered?" Mabel asked.

"Hey. Lady. That wasn't my fault. There's only so much a man can do if he's not actually living in the place. I did chase off those punks who broke the windows, but—"

"Never mind. Look. I went in here earlier because I heard that cat crying. She seemed to be injured, and we'd like to check on her and get her some help if we can."

He looked them over and apparently decided Mabel and Lisa were harmless and well-intentioned. "Well, ya can't get into the house till the cops clear it, anyway."

"We were just checking the hedges. She might not be able to get back up there with an injured leg," Lisa said.

"Couldn't we just check these last few bushes?" Mabel asked.

He considered. "I guess it wouldn't hurt any. Just stay outside the tape, okay?"

"Of course." Mabel eyed him. "Have you talked to the Gundersens yet about what happened today?"

"Hoo-boy." He rolled his eyes. "They just about went nuts—somebody getting killed right in their house."

"You saw the body, right? Did you recognize the guy?"

"Naw. Probably just a break-in. Somebody who didn't know the place was completely empty."

"Would you mind if we stopped for a minute after we check for the cat? I've been staying over on Carteret with my grandma. She just had a hip replacement, and she doesn't know much about this house or who lived there. Just curious to know more about the place."

"I guess that would be okay. Gets pretty lonely now the wife's gone."

"Oh, I'm so sorry!"

The man stared at Mabel. "She's not dead. She's in Wisconsin, visiting her sister."

"Oh, that's good." Mabel giggled awkwardly. "Heard it was nice up there in the summer."

"Too many bugs," he said. "Just stop by. I'll be on my porch."

***

Of course, though they made a complete circuit of the bushes, there was no sign of the cat. The ham aroma rising from Mabel's fanny pack was starting to appeal. "You want to split it?"

"Ew, no."

"It's wrapped up. It's what we just had for dinner."

"Doesn't matter. It's my policy to never eat fanny-pack cat meat."

They returned to the sidewalk and headed toward Mower Man's porch. "What if he offers us a drink or something?" Lisa hissed.

"I hope so. That ham was delicious, but it always makes me thirsty."

Lisa caught her arm. "Did it ever occur to you that guy might know more about that body than he's letting on? That man has a key to the house—he wouldn't have to climb through a window to kill somebody."

Mabel swallowed. "Good point. Okay, we don't accept any snacks."

"And we do not, under any circumstances, go inside."

"Right. Porch only."

The man was still waiting, as promised, on a white-painted Adirondack chair. A pitcher of lemonade and three glasses stood on the table next to it. "Lemonade?" he called down as they approached. "It's from one of those mixes—no calories."

Mabel considered the trickle of moisture making its way down the cool condensation on the pitcher surface and swallowed again. She was so thirsty. "No, thank you."

Mower Man didn't bother getting up when Mabel and Lisa came up the steps. Maybe he hadn't been raised right, or maybe he just couldn't hop up out of that low-riding seat.

Lisa sat on the broad porch railing, next to the steps, likely for strategic reasons. Mabel accepted the other Adirondack chair and quickly regretted it. Now she would be the one with her backside stuck in a chair.

Mower Man took a long drink of his lemonade, gazing out over his freshly trimmed front lawn, now lit by a parade of solar walkway lights and a twinkling of fireflies. Reclining with drink in hand, wearing his yellow Hawaiian-print board shorts and white beater shirt, he looked like a man for whom all was right in the world.

He turned his head at a loud buzzing sound. "Got another one," he cackled, gesturing toward the bug zapper attached to the edge of the porch roof.

"You know those kill a lot of good bugs." Lisa went into teacher mode. "Bugs we all need to have around."

He rolled his eyes exaggeratedly. "You sound like the wife. I don't want to get chewed up by a bunch of bugs when I sit out. My house, my rules."

The zapper buzzed again. Mabel gritted her teeth. It was going to be hard to ignore the sound of frying bugs every few seconds.

"So what can I do for you?" he asked.

"Well, I guess first we ought to introduce ourselves. I'm Mabel Browne and this is Lisa Benedetti."

"Hey."

"And you are?"

"Pete." No last name forthcoming, and the morning's introductions had fled her brain the moment they happened. At least, now Mabel wouldn't have to keep thinking of him as Mower Man.

"Hi, Pete. So you didn't know the dead guy. Did the neighbor with the spatula recognize him?"

"That's Carlo. Him and his wife just moved here from Pittsburgh a year ago. They don't know anybody."

"How about the Gundersens? Did anyone send them a picture to ID?"

"I don't know. The police didn't say anything, and I sure wasn't taking pictures."

"How long did you live next to the Gundersens?"

"Oh ..." He appeared to think, staring at the porch ceiling. "Maybe twenty years or so. I was already here when they moved in. They asked me to keep an eye on things after they moved a couple of years ago. Wish now I hadn'ta said yes."

"I'm surprised they didn't sell the place." Lisa slid to her feet, apparently having trouble staying comfortable on the railing.

"They had grandkids somewhere. Think they had some idea one of the kids might want to move here one day. Or maybe they'd turn it into a rental."

Mabel was thinking of the complexities of letting a vacant house sit around for two years. Insurance on an unoccupied house could be steep. Then, you had the risk of vandalism, frozen pipes, roof leaks. Not to mention dead bodies.

"Who had it before the Gundersens?"

"Armbrusters. They were here probably fifteen years or so. Just them and their boy. Kid was kind of a pain. Me and the wife were never blessed. We're not used to all the yelling and stuff. Anyway, nice family, other than the noise. Least once the kid moved out. He was always in some kinda trouble. They spoiled him 'cause he was an only child."

Mabel avoided Lisa's eyes, hoping she wouldn't go on one of her rants about people without kids or training who spewed opinions about child-rearing.

Pete seemed oblivious to Lisa's glare. "Gundersens were a lot quieter. They had teenage girls."

"Do they have any ideas?" Lisa's determination to investigate won out. She eased into the third Adirondack chair. As short as she was, her feet stuck out several inches above the floor.

"'Bout the dead guy? Nah. Phil was having fits, trying to figure out how somebody got in, in the first place. He was already hot about all the broken windows. Didn't come right out and say so, but it sure sounded like he blamed me. Like I should guard the place 24/7? Like I should sit out there with a shotgun or something?"

"Of course, it wasn't your fault." Lisa's kindergarten-teacher voice was back. "Are they going to return since this happened?"

"Didn't say." Pete mopped his damp, graying forelock back from his brow. "What a mess."

"How do you think the guy got in there?" Mabel asked. "Did anyone else have the key?"

"Nope." Pete stopped with his glass halfway to his mouth. "Hey, are you insinuating …?"

"Not at all!" Mabel hastily assured him. "Just thought if somebody else maybe had a key, that would have been the easiest way into the house." *Certainly a lot easier than scaling the outside wall like a cat burglar.* That thought reminded Mabel of the little cat. She hoped she was okay.

"I wish I did know of somebody. You're right. It would be easier. But as far as I know the only people with keys are me and them." He frowned. "And their girls, I guess. But they don't live around here."

"Do you think …?" Lisa leaned forward. Or, at least, she made the attempt before the Adirondack chair defeated her.

"I wouldn't think so. I mean, why? They're nice girls … I guess. I don't know them all that well. They minded their own business when they lived here. I liked that."

"Where are they living now — do you know?" Mabel asked.

"Um, one's up in Schenectady — or maybe Skaneateles. One of those complicated New York towns with an S. She's a college professor. Married. Other one's still in PA, but more toward Harrisburg. Think she might still be single. Don't know what she does for a living."

"Other than them, nobody else you can think of?"

Pete shook his head. "I'll think about it, though. You better believe the cops will be asking."

"Is there any other way into the house you can think of?" Lisa asked.

Just then, the phone rang somewhere inside.

"That'll be the wife. I didn't tell her yet—she won't believe this one."

Pete leveraged his body from the chair. "Got a live trap you can use for your cat if you want. I drug it out for you." He nodded toward the shadows at the other side of the porch.

Without a goodbye, he disappeared inside the house, letting the screen door bang shut behind him. "I'm coming," he grumbled.

"Thank you," Mabel called after him. She collected the wooden trap, which looked homemade, as well as somewhat grimy and cobwebby, and limped as she made her way to the steps. "I think I pulled something, getting up."

Behind her, Lisa was still kicking her short legs, trying to extricate herself from the chair's grip. Finally, she launched, trotted a couple steps, and stumbled into Mabel.

"It's a real mystery, Mabes. And you're in the middle of it."

"The only mystery I'm interested in is where that cat went and whether she's okay."

"Well, now we've got a trap for your cat, and we learned a lot too," Lisa chirped. "What I call a good night's work!"

Mabel laid a hand on Lisa's wrist. "Yeah, it was. But I mean it. You and I aren't the Dana Girls. Let's concentrate on the kitty and leave detecting to the people who are trained to do it."

"Well, sure. But this is the twenty-first century. Citizen detectives can do a lot of things nowadays."

Mabel trudged toward the street. "Get arrested. Get killed. Screw up a police investigation. Help a criminal escape."

"Pfft. Not people who know what they're doing. We can actually help the police." Lisa launched into an account of a serial killer, captured thanks to the group she referred to as "citizen detectives" with laptops.

"Maybe ..." Of course, those people had been working with the police. And computer research sounded nice and safe. If she could track the killer from the security of her kitchen, maybe being a citizen detective wouldn't be too bad. Maybe it would be kind of exciting.

Chapter Seven

The morning dawned cool, despite the predicted scorcher. Mabel helped Grandma out onto the front porch with her newspaper, phone, and coffee. She assured Mabel she could get back inside with no problem if she needed to. "Stop hovering, baby. You can help with laundry when you get back if that makes you feel better."

"Call me if there's anything at all. I'm not going very far," Mabel told her, as Grandma waved her off.

The dew still sparkled on the grass as Mabel made her way up the street. In front of the Sauer mansion, orange daylilies lifted their faces to the sun.

She would check the live trap in hopes the little cat would be in it and could be retrieved before the day got too hot. Mabel figured if she was anywhere in the vicinity, she'd have smelled the ham they'd used as bait.

The neighbor's house lay quiet. Mabel wondered if Pete was a late sleeper. If she saw him, she'd press him a bit more about other ways to get inside the house. Somehow, two people had gotten in there with or without a key—the victim and his murderer. Assuming it had been a murder.

Mabel shuddered. Hopefully, the police would make a statement about that soon. At least once the medical examiner had finished the autopsy.

She and Lisa had tucked the baited live trap into the bushes between the murder house and Pete's yard, with the opening angled toward the back of the house and the window Mabel had crawled through. Mabel had been proud of the way they'd camouflaged it with the hedge branches.

As she slipped along the side of the house, Mabel caught sight of the trap. Hallelujah—the door flap was down. Of course, the trap might've been sprung and still be empty, but the closed door was a hopeful sign, at least.

She hurried her steps, wishing too late she'd made a plan for capturing the kitty once the trap was opened. If she wasn't careful, she'd lose the cat a second time and probably make her all the warier.

As Mabel crept up on the trap, she decided. The cat was small, and Mabel wasn't too far from home—only four blocks or so. If the cat was inside, she would carry the entire trap home, and then open it in Grandma's spare bedroom.

Mabel crouched down and stretched a tentative hand toward the box trap. Her sweater brushed the leaves and dew rained onto her arm. *Yuck.* She rubbed her damp sleeve in vain before finally rolling it up.

Something moved inside the wooden trap. *Yes.* Again, Mabel reached out and grabbed the handle.

Oh, my. Surely, the cat wasn't this heavy? Mabel couldn't imagine carrying this weight all the way back to Grandma's. Four blocks—one of them her own very long block—didn't seem like a short walk anymore.

Maybe she'd try to take the tiniest peek, and if the cat was in there, she might convince Pete to carry it inside his garage or somewhere she could hope to transfer her to an actual carrier. Then, Mabel could come back with the car. She'd have to have it anyway if the kitty needed a vet.

And if this *wasn't* the cat, the sooner she found it out and released the poor thing, the better.

Mind resolved, Mabel shifted her tired legs, cramping from her crouched position, and tipped the front of the trap up. She eased the door flap back to make a narrow crack at the bottom so she could peer in.

The instant the crack opened, a narrow snout appeared, showing savage, pointed yellow teeth. The snarling mouth was followed by a claw-like, almost human hand, prying at the flap. Then another terrifying set of claws appeared, grabbing for Mabel, as the creature released a guttural growl.

It was breaking through the narrow opening.

Mabel scrambled backward, dropping the trap and struggling to get her stiff legs under her. Painful pins and needles shot up the numb pair of stumps she'd formerly known as her calves.

She was crawling away now, desperate to get to safety.

The animal burst forth, charging directly at her.

Why wasn't it running back into the bushes? Whatever that creature was, Mabel was now sure it must be rabid. That thought penetrated the dead nerves in her legs and she shot to her feet,

"Help! Mr...." *Darn.* What was his name? "Pete!"

Mabel tripped, caught herself, and looked back. A raccoon. And it was gaining.

She raced for the front sidewalk. That ... thing ...was enormous. If one believed the internet videos, raccoons were adorable, the almost-human clowns of the animal world.

Mabel would never believe anything she saw on the internet ever again.

She reached the sidewalk, tripped over the curb, and sprawled on her hands and knees. "Mr. Pete!" she shrieked. "Help! He's after me!"

Pete ran from his house, barefoot and dressed only in Valentine pajama pants covered in fat cupids. His hair stood up as if he'd just rolled out of bed at Mabel's screams.

"I'm coming!" He brandished a broom like a club. "Where is he?"

Mabel pointed, but the raccoon had vanished.

Pete vaulted the hedge with surprising agility and ran toward the back of the Gundersen house. Mabel rolled over and sat, gasping for air. She examined her hands and knees, brushing off the dirt and picking bits of gravel out of the scrapes. Nothing seemed to be bleeding, but she was going to be sore.

Moments later, Pete returned, breathing hard. "No sign of him." This time, he walked around the hedge. "Did you get a good look at him? I mean like to describe him?"

Mabel couldn't imagine why it mattered. "I didn't really spend a lot of time looking at him. I was running away. He had the usual mask, of course."

"No kidding?"

She tried not to roll her eyes. After all, Pete *had* come to her rescue. "Yeah. No kidding. His hair was shaggy and sort of gray-brown. And he had evil eyes and pointy yellow teeth."

"You poor kid. I believe you, but things do look worse when we're scared." Pete patted her shoulder. "Big guy?"

"He had to be over thirty pounds."

"Huh?" Pete straightened and stared. "You were attacked by a vicious toddler?"

Mabel grimaced as the picture became clear. She rubbed her forehead. "No. I'm so sorry ... I didn't mean to give you the impression a person was attacking me. It was a huge raccoon."

As Pete continued to stare, Mabel blurted, "I think he was rabid."

Pete lowered the broom he'd still been clenching in his right hand. He doubled over, hands on his knees, and drew some deep breaths. "Nearly gave myself a heart attack. Thought it was the murderer."

"I know. I realize that now, and I'm so sorry."

He straightened back up, muttering something under his breath. "No problem. Any luck with your cat?"

She shook her head. "The raccoon was in the trap. He stole the bait."

"That's too bad. Well, you're welcome to leave it where it sits and try again tonight, if you want."

"Thanks. Now I'm a little bit scared of that raccoon coming back."

Pete scratched his grizzled chin. "Tell you what. Set it if you want, and in the morning, I'll check it for you."

"Thanks. That would be great."

"But you know what? As soon as the police clear the house, you can go in and look. I need to get those second-floor windows boarded up anyway. The last thing I want is to board the cat up inside."

"I hope she's okay that long. She did look like she was hurt."

***

Her brush with the killer raccoon had left Mabel shaken and ravenously hungry. She decided the best thing she could do next was stop at the Coffee Cup Diner and clean her wounds. Her mouth watered. She'd have loved a big Farmhand Breakfast, but Grandma would be waiting and wondering where she was. Reluctantly, Mabel decided to be satisfied with an extra-large Coconut Island frozen latte and a few pastries to take home and share with Grandma Mabel.

The diner bustled with breakfast traffic, and the smells of bacon and coffee nearly made Mabel swoon like a southern belle with a thirty-two-inch waist and an eighteen-inch corset. *Be strong.* She elbowed her way to the end of the counter where takeout menus sat in a napkin holder.

After waiting a few minutes for the older waitress to finish chatting with the guys in feed caps at the other end of the counter, Mabel watched her distribute a couple checks and refill coffees. Finally, she made eye contact.

"Help you, honey?"

Mabel placed her order, then waved her gritty hands. "I'll be back to pick that up as soon as I wash this off."

The waitress, the pin on whose pink uniform read "Patti," frowned. "You're bleeding, hon. You take a fall?"

Mabel laughed airily. "Just a little tumble. I'm okay."

She'd now attracted attention from the people crowding the counter and standing in line. Ducking her head, Mabel threaded her way to the short back hallway where the restrooms were located. Both knees were now stinging and feeling stiff, but her hopes of darting inside and quickly cleaning up were dashed by the line of women waiting for a single restroom.

At least the hall was dimly lit, and her fellow bathroom-seekers seemed too absorbed in their chatter to pay Mabel any attention. She leaned back against the wall, letting the female voices swirl around her.

At first she wasn't really paying attention, but soon, fragments of conversation penetrated. "Bugmann ..." *Or was it "bug man"?*

"It was Carl Schuster ..."

"... think it had to have something to do with those burglaries—no, really!"

"I never trusted him."

The conversations ceased when the next-to-last person entered the restroom. Mabel itched to ask the remaining woman what they'd all been talking about but couldn't think of a polite way to do it.

Finally, she tapped the shoulder of the woman ahead of her. The woman, a husky pony-tailed blonde in denim capris and an American flag T-shirt, turned.

"Excuse me. I couldn't help overhearing. I just wondered—"

The door opened and the blonde excused herself. "Yeah," she tossed over her shoulder. "They're saying it was that creep, Carl Schuster."

Mabel silently repeated the name a couple times. A creep, was he? The name meant nothing to her, but she'd ask Grandma when she got home.

***

Mabel recognized Ms. Katherine Ann's big red Cadillac Eldorado in Grandma's driveway when she got home. Excited female voices and laughter floated through the house's open windows.

Mabel pulled off her sunglasses as she entered the dark kitchen and shoved Barnacle's inquiring nose away from the bag of pastries. "Hello? I'm home."

"There she is! Come on in here."

Miss Birdie resembled an unnourished bumblebee in school-bus yellow spandex tank top and black-and-yellow spandex shorts, perching on the arm of the overstuffed sofa. Ms. Katherine Ann, wearing a billowy red gingham sundress, sat in the lounger opposite Grandma's kitchen chair.

Grandma's eyes lit up at the Coffee Cup bag. "Did you bring us something good?"

Mabel opened the bag and held it out. "I got a variety, so there's enough for everybody."

As she passed the treats around, Grandma licked chocolate off her fingers. "Thank you, baby. That hits the spot."

"We were just discussing your murder." Ms. Katherine Anne gestured to the morning paper lying on Grandma's table, using her cruller as a pointer.

"Ohhh …" Mabel set her now-sweating frozen drink on a coaster and pounced on the newspaper. "They were talking about this down at the diner. Somebody called the victim—this Carl guy—a creep."

"You could ask Katherine about that." Grandma's voice was dry. "Is there another chocolate in there, baby?"

Mabel fleetingly considered Grandma's nutritional needs but decided in this case the endorphin boost was worth it. She passed another chocolate-glazed doughnut and took a Napoleon for herself. Mabel's endorphins needed a boost too.

Ms. Katherine Ann raised both arms in the air and shook her head. "Don't get me started again. I just got my blood pressure back down."

Grandma snorted. "You've been complaining about that guy for years. Once more probably won't kill you."

"Guess my heart can take it." Ms. Katherine Ann leaned forward, bringing the foot of the recliner down with a whoosh. "Okay, here goes. So every year, I get this infestation in my front hallway. It's like hundreds of teeny tiny little ants with wings. They come crawling up from along the baseboard and swarm all over the glass in the front door. They—"

"She doesn't need their whole life cycle, Katherine." Miss Birdie rolled her eyes over the rim of her coffee cup.

"You want me to tell it, I'll tell it my own way. So they stink something awful. It's those feminine hormones they release."

Mabel frowned. "Pheromones?"

"It doesn't matter. Are there any more chocolate?" Grandma craned to check the bag.

"All gone. Sorry."

"So I used to get a guy in from Bartles Grove every spring to spray for them. He said they were harmless—just nasty to live with for a few days every year. But then this exterminator place opened up over here, and I figured I'd give 'em a try. Support local, you know?"

Mabel nodded, totally lost.

"Had been seeing the van around town—white van with Bug Man painted on the side."

"And a man-size dead bug on its back on the roof." Miss Birdie, amazingly flexible for her age, dropped back onto the couch to demonstrate bug legs in the air.

"Mm-hmm." Grandma wiggled her pointer fingers on either side of her head. "And these huge antennas bobbing around on the front of the van roof."

"But I don't get—"

Ms. Katherine Ann held up a hand. "I'm just getting to it, baby. So I call him up, right? And he makes an appointment to come out next morning. I wait and wait. Birdie and I were supposed to do our power walk, but I have this appointment with the exterminator, so I wait.

Then my hairdresser has a cancellation, and could have took me in early, but no ... I've got to wait."

Ms. Birdie sat back up. "He never showed."

Ms. Katherine Ann glared at her friend. "Like I said, I was getting to that. He never showed."

"Ever again," Grandma said. "No more Bug Man."

"Wait." Mabel felt as if she was finally catching up to the narrative. "The Bug Man was Carl? The dead guy?"

Chapter Eight

C arl Schuster was the Bug Man." Ms. Katherine Ann spoke slowly and clearly. "This is what I'm trying to tell you. He disappeared. His van disappeared. And now he turns up dead in a vacant house. I couldn't get anybody to come out and spray, so my house was overrun with those horrible flying ants. I had to do it myself."

The anger puzzled Mabel. "Well, if he was dead, no wonder he couldn't come spray your house."

"No," Ms. Katherine Ann insisted, "it was the burglaries. The man was a crook on the lam. He just happened to get caught."

Mabel had been standing, but decided it was time to sit on the end of the unoccupied hospital bed. "What burglaries?"

Miss Birdie sighed. "I don't blame you for being confused, baby. It's a good thing Katherine don't drive in the big city. She'd be jumping sidewalks on both sides the street. Long story short. There was a string of burglaries around town awhile back. After a bit, people figured out a bunch of them were in places the Bug Man had been in to exterminate."

"They stopped when the Bug Man disappeared," Grandma said.

"Obviously, Bug Man no-showed the wrong person." Ms. Katherine Ann folded her arms stubbornly.

"I thought it was the burglaries." Mabel's head spun.

Ms. Katherine Ann huffed air through her frizzy bangs. "Why was he in a vacant house? Obviously, he didn't know they moved everything out. Probably got called to exorcise the place before the people moved out, and he never showed. Came back after the people were gone, to clean the place out — and I don't mean bugs! They caught him and got into a tussle because they couldn't sell the place, thanks to him."

Mabel shook her head once in an attempt to settle Ms. Katherine Ann's theory into some sort of logical order but failed.

"I'll bet you once the police look into it, they're gonna find that place full of termites," Ms. Katherine Ann predicted.

"The bug van went missing too." Miss Birdie calmly turned the conversation back.

"Well, it sounds distinctive enough that somebody ought to be able to spot it." Mabel reached into the pastry bag and withdrew an empty hand coated with powdered sugar and a smear of raspberry jelly. *Darn.* Barnacle offered to help with the clean-up, and she nudged him aside.

Miss Birdie shrugged. "Doubt anybody was even looking for it. Not then. Rumor mill said the bug company was involved in all those burglaries. His partner claimed the guy was skimming profits. Plenty of reasons for him just to run off, but not anything you'd put out an APB for."

"Probably easy to change that van up," Grandma said. "There any more chocolate ones, Mabel?"

"No," Mabel repeated. "Sorry."

Grandma sighed. "All you'd need to do,'" she said, "was take off that dead bug and the antennas. Maybe change the paint job."

Mabel excused herself as the old ladies got into a complicated discussion of chop shops and stolen license plates, comparing information gleaned from old episodes of *The Rockford Files* and other long-defunct crime shows. She carried the empty pastry bag to the kitchen trash container, closely followed by Barnacle's eager nose and slobbering jaws.

As she washed her sticky hands at the sink, she thought about what she'd managed to learn, despite the ladies' conversational detours. The main thing that stood out was that the missing Bug Man had turned up dead in the vacant Gundersen house, but his very distinctive missing van was still unaccounted for. *How? Why? Where?*

"Come on. Let's go for a walk." Mabel's involvement with the late Bug Man was over, she told herself firmly. She clipped the leash to Barnacle's collar and headed outside, but the questions still swirled through her head.

***

"This is creepy." Lisa snapped a picture of the staircase with her cell phone. "Exciting and creepy." The police had finally cleared the house, and Pete had entrusted Mabel with the key.

"It's just an old house," Mabel told her, more to convince herself than Lisa. "It does feel weird being in here, though, coming right up the steps instead of scaling the fire escape."

With all the lower windows boarded over, shadows cloaked the stairs. The electricity had been turned off, as Mabel had discovered when she'd flipped the switch. Only a couple pale streaks of sunlight from the upper floor highlighted the top steps.

"This is it." Mabel stood back and gestured toward the murder room, struck by a sudden quiver of nerves.

Lisa angled past her and stepped into the center of the now-empty room. She turned in a slow circle, holding her phone in front of her. "I am in the murder room," she said, stating the obvious. The phone jerked. "Oh, hey, is that blood?"

Mabel pushed the phone down. "Yes, of course, it's blood. Are you videoing?"

"Just for evidence purposes." Lisa bent and examined the dark, rusty blotches on the floor where Carl Schuster's head had rested. She started to raise her phone, caught Mabel's eye, and lowered it again. "The police did clear the house, didn't they?"

"Yeah, but apparently the blood is the homeowner's problem. Pete said the police gave him a number to call for a crime-scene cleanup company."

Mabel set the live trap near the broken window, figuring the little cat might be using that as her point of entry. "Here's some more blood on the sill, but I'm betting that belongs to the kitty."

Lisa peered over her shoulder. "How do you think the vic and whoever killed him got in?"

Mabel shrugged and gestured behind her. "I honestly don't know, but maybe the same way I did. Through the window in the room across the hall."

"I saw the dead guy's picture—not dead, you know, just his picture. And he looked kind of chunky to be climbing up the sides of houses and squeezing through windows."

Mabel opened her mouth, then closed it. It was actually sort of flattering that Lisa didn't think Mabel was too plump to play human fly. Spandex really helped in these situations. Most situations, when you came right down to it.

Lisa pulled her shirt away from her back. "It's stifling in here."

"Well, it's ninety out and the place is mostly closed up. Let's set the trap and get out of here." Mabel pulled out a baggie with slivers of chicken in it.

"I'm just going to walk around quick while you do that, okay?"

Lisa left, apparently intent on checking out the approach from the fire escape via the bedroom across the hall, and Mabel hurried to set the trap. After the raccoon incident, she'd abandoned the old wooden trap for a new wire mesh one she'd borrowed from the Medicine Spring animal shelter. From now on, she planned to see what she was dealing with.

As soon as the trap was set, she climbed back onto her feet and looked around the room one last time. She presumed the police had removed samples of the blood and probably taken a bunch of crime scene photos. Surprisingly, she saw no chalk outline on the floor. She'd have to ask Lisa about that since she was more up on police procedure than Mabel ever wanted to be.

She shut her eyes, trying to remember details from her last time here. She couldn't pinpoint anything different other than no body this time. And no candy wrappers. They'd likely be testing those for fingerprints or DNA or something.

Her footsteps echoed off the bare, gray-painted wood floor. A rectangular area in the center of the room, about eight by ten feet, stood out in a darker gray.

Lisa appeared in the doorway. "You find something?"

"No. Just looking at that dark section of floor." She pointed. "Thinking there must've been a rug here once, but the floor was bare when I found the body. The Gundersens most likely rolled up the rug and took it with them when they moved. You see anything?"

Lisa shook her head. "You found the cat back there?" She jerked a thumb at the room across the hall.

"In the closet, yeah. But it ran through here and must've gone out the broken window. I heard the sound of falling glass."

"Why would it do that?"

"I think the poor thing just ran for an opening. The window must've already been broken—the cat just broke off a bit more glass on its way out."

Lisa took a picture of the broken window. "No person could've fit through there."

"Agreed. Let's get out of here."

As they emerged into the sunlight again, Mabel took a moment to relock the door.

"Hey, ladies!" Pete the neighbor was at the curb in front of his house, pulling his newspaper out of the delivery box. "You get your trap set?"

"We did, thanks." Mabel handed him the house key. "Quick question. Do you think that bedroom window got broken when the guy—Schuster—was killed?"

"Nah." He shook his head. "Windows were all solid till we got all that vandalism down on the first floor, and that was pretty recent. From what I saw—not that I'm no expert—but I think Schuster was there awhile. Seems like if he was killed around the time he disappeared, that was way before the windows happened."

"Do you have any idea why he was in that house?"

Pete swatted at a bee with the newspaper. "None at all. It was weird too because he'd been there before. What are the odds?"

"On a job or …?"

"Oh, it was a job all right. Not all that long before Gundersens left. A few months? They called him in for fleas."

"No problems with that, I guess?" Mabel asked.

Pete snorted. "Yeah … You might say there were problems."

Lisa poked Mabel in the side, making her yelp.

"Did a bee get ya?" Pete motioned for them to follow him to the porch. "They're all through that patch of clover."

"Mmm," Mabel said noncommittally. She glared at Lisa as they trailed Pete up the walkway and gave her a reply jab.

"They. Had. Problems," Lisa hissed.

"I. Heard. That," Mabel hissed back.

Pete motioned them to sit. "Gonna be another hot one."

Mabel agreed. Yes, it was definitely going to be another hot one. "So what exactly happened between Schuster and your neighbors? If you don't mind my asking."

"Hoo-ee!" He rolled his eyes. "Fleas. They had fleas. Margie drug home cats all the time. Even Phil couldn't take it no more. He told me once, he said, 'Pete, Margie's a good woman and you know I love 'er, but she needs to quit with the dang cats.' You know once they had like fifteen cats in that place. Sometimes when the wind was just right, you could catch a whiff all the way over here. And Phil, he said, he'd find cat hair right in his—"

"Wow," Lisa cut the story hour short. "That sounds like a nightmare, all right. You say they had fleas?"

"The whole house. They tried everything. They sprayed the house. They gave those cats flea dip. You ever try to give a cat a flea dip? It sure ain't pretty. Phil, he had scratches like you wouldn't believe. Fifteen cats. The screechin' was something awful."

"So they called the Bug Man?" Mabel hinted.

"Yeah, they saw his ad on the TV, and Marge, she was all for it. Seemed like he could cure just about any kind of infestation according to that ad. Did you ever see those ads?"

Mabel started to shake her head, but quickly stopped herself when she realized this would likely lead to a lengthy description of the ads in question. "Um. I take it they hired him. Was he successful?"

"He fumigated the whole darn house. Phil and Marge, they had to go away overnight and lock all them cats in the basement while they were gone. Watched from my porch. He set out a bunch of bomb things all over the house, and then run through, top to bottom, wearing a mask and setting them off." Pete cackled. "For a guy on the plump side, he sure could run."

"But it didn't work?" Lisa prompted.

"No, ma'am. It did not. So they had to do the whole darn thing over again. And what do you know? They still had fleas."

"Oh, dear." Mabel scratched herself. All this flea talk was making her itchy.

"So this caused a dispute?" Lisa asked.

"A dispute? You might say that. Each time the Bug Man came in to fumigate it run close to $500, as it's a pretty big house, as you can see."

"That seems like a lot," Mabel said.

"That's what they thought, but he caught 'em desperate, and he was the only company near here. They were already pretty mad when it didn't work the first time around. Phil even speculated it was a scam, makin' them bring him in a second time."

"Did it work that time?" Lisa asked.

He shook his head. "Still crawling with fleas and gettin' bit. After chargin' them all that money. Plus, of course, they had to pay for a hotel twice. So they flat refused to pay."

"How did that work out?" Mabel guessed it hadn't.

"Ended up in front of the magistrate. They insisted he was a rip-off artist, trying to extort money from them. He claimed they were deadbeats, that he did the work, and it was their fault it didn't work because they never had those cats treated by a vet."

"What did the court do?" Lisa asked.

"She cut the baby in half because it was all a lot of finger pointing and not much proof either way. Ordered 'em to pay him half."

"How'd that go?" By this point, Mabel was enjoying the story.

"Like you'd figure. Nobody was happy. Everybody was mad. Out in the parking lot afterward, the Bug Man made a remark about the cats, and Margie took a swing at him. And then he called her a … a name, so Phil jumped on him and wrestled him to the ground."

"No kidding? Wow." Mabel glanced over at Lisa who was jiggling her foot with excitement. She must feel, as Mabel did, that the Gundersens were looking a lot like suspects. And Ms. Katherine Ann was right. The whole thing went back to bugs. Who'd have believed it?

Pete, lost in his story, didn't seem to notice Mabel and Lisa's reaction. "Not that Phil could blame the guy too much for his remarks. Phil wasn't too crazy about the cats himself, and he knew for sure they hadn't treated them like they were supposed to. I mean, who can afford the vet for fifteen cats?

"He was just mad about the money. And covered in these big, itchy welts—you shoulda seen 'em." Pete looked off toward the neighboring house. "Phil's got a temper. And when the Bug Man insulted Margie, it gave Phil an excuse to lay into him."

Chapter Nine

Mabel followed Pete's glance toward the murder house. His gaze was unfocused as if thinking about all that had happened and not really looking at anything in particular.

But Mabel's eyes were instantly drawn to a small creature, slinking through the overgrown grass. Pete, seeming to notice her attention to the neighboring yard, cleared his throat.

"I plan on cutting that grass later today. It's one of the things I take care of over there. Just too hot for a man my age to cut two big lawns in one day, and then the police closed it all off."

"No. I mean that's good. But hey, no judgment. I was looking at the cat, see?" Mabel stood and pointed. "She's going back toward the house. You think she's still limping?"

"Hard to tell," Pete said. "You goin' after her?"

"No. She'd only run. I'm just going to pray the trap works." Mabel frowned as she watched the little cat. "Did the Gundersens take all the cats when they moved?"

"No way. Phil said he wasn't trucking fifteen cats to Arizona just to get caught up in all that again. Margie took three of them, and they found homes for the rest."

"You think she might be offspring of one of theirs?" Mabel nodded at the little cat.

He rubbed his chin. "Well, I guess it could be. Could easily be one or two got away in the confusion and reproduced. They didn't say nothin' to me, but a lot was going on right then. What you planning on doing with it, if you catch it?"

Mabel raised one shoulder in a shrug. "Take her to the vet, anyway. Look for her owner."

"That's the smart thing. Think about where cats led Margie over there. No place good."

***

"Can I give you a ride?" Lisa nodded at her car, parked in front of Pete's house.

Mabel knew she could easily walk home, but it was already getting hot. "Sure."

As soon as they got in, Lisa turned on the AC, and they pulled away from the curb. But she drove off in the wrong direction.

"Hey, where are you going?"

"To talk to the Bug Man's partner, of course." Lisa consulted her map app as they waited at a light. "Get his side of the story."

"Come on. I need to get back to Grandma's. We're not the police. How are we supposed to question somebody about something that's none of our business?"

Lisa smiled and accelerated. "Watch and learn, grasshopper."

Great. Mabel slumped back in her seat. She'd been kidnapped. But—she had to admit—also curious.

If Lisa had had any concerns about finding the Bug Man's shop, she needn't have worried. Even someone with zero command of the English language could've identified the nature of the business from the giant dead bug painted in garish green and red on the front awning. As Miss Birdie had described, it lay on its back, legs in the air and antennas drooping.

As Lisa pulled into a metered space out front, Mabel didn't move to unbuckle her seatbelt.

"C'mon. This will only take a minute."

Mabel sighed. "Just what, exactly, do you plan on asking this guy?"

Lisa was already outside, plugging the meter.

Mabel got out realizing Lisa was going into the shop with or without her. This seemed foolish, but Mabel was nothing if not loyal.

A bell above the door ding-donged to announce their arrival.

"May I help you?" A bald man, maybe in his early forties, appeared in the doorway to the back of the shop and removed dark-framed glasses to squint at them. He had the body of a professional wrestler, muscles bulging against his white-and-green Bug Man T-shirt.

"Hi, there." Lisa bubbled right up to him and stuck out her right hand. "Are you the Bug Man?"

He shifted his glasses to his left hand and shook. "Martin Hernandez. You have a pest problem?"

"Lisa Benedetti. Yes. Um. Bees," she said. "In the clover."

Hernandez leaned back against the countertop and polished his glasses on the bottom of his T-shirt. "Bees, huh? You know what kind?"

Lisa's hands fluttered. "Oh, you know. They have stripes. They buzz."

Mabel had to turn around and pretend to study the bug posters on the wall to hide her massive eye roll.

Hernandez cleared his throat. "That actually covers quite a bit of territory, Miss." He replaced his glasses on the bridge of his nose. "You got bumblebees, honeybees, yellowjackets, carpenter bees, mason bees, wasps, hoverflies — which aren't bees, but people always think they are—"

69

"How about maybe honeybees?" Lisa's voice rose with a note of uncertainty.

"But you're not sure, right? Listen. If they're outside in the clover, they're most likely just honeybees. They're struggling right now with colony collapse, and they're important to crop pollination and making honey. We don't want to kill them. What we do is try and relocate them. But unless you've got a swarm somewhere, that isn't much of a solution. Now, if you want to look at some pictures—"

"No, you know what? They're actually in a friend's yard. Maybe I'll talk to him first, okay? I could get a picture?"

The guy nodded. He wore a bland, agreeable expression, but Mabel got the clear impression he heard this sort of vague rambling every day.

"Do you have a price list?" Lisa delivered the sort of charming smile that made Hernandez smile back. Mabel's smiles didn't carry the same power.

"I'm sorry." He shook his head. "There's too much variation, depending on what it is, where it's at, how bad the infestation is … But once I come out, I can give you an estimate."

"Okay. I'll give you a call." Lisa's gaze roved around the small storefront. "Hey," she said, in the bemused tone of somebody who's just had a random thought, "by the way, is Carl around?"

Hernandez's eyes narrowed. Maybe not in outright suspicion, but with a definite air of calculation. "Do you know Carl? I'm sorry to be the one to tell you. Carl is deceased."

"Oh, no!" Lisa's eyes widened, and she gathered the front of her shirt in a convincing display of shock and distress. "No, I don't. Didn't. He just did a job for my friend's neighbor and I thought I'd look him up."

She had been the star of their middle school plays, and Mabel had to admit Lisa still had Broadway potential. Or at least off-Broadway. But Mabel broke in. She no longer had the patience to wait for the second act of this impromptu drama. "I saw something in the news. His body was just discovered in a vacant building, wasn't it?"

"Yeah." Hernandez's voice carried no apparent regret. "No ruling from the coroner yet, but I'll bet you he was up to nothing good in that place. I'm still getting complaints on the guy. Guessing that might be why you wanted to talk to him?"

Hernandez didn't wait for their answer. "When the van disappeared along with him awhile back, I figured he skipped town."

"I'm so sorry," Mabel said. "Were you in business together a long time?"

"Nah. He joined me two-three years ago, and I wish I'd never met him. He handled our taxes. Supposedly. Well, they were never paid. Now, he gets himself killed, and the books don't add up either."

Chapter Ten

Mabel handed Grandma her sweet tea and a coaster. The last load of laundry was tumbling in the dryer. "Is there anything else you need right now?"

Grandma hit the mute button as an Ensure commercial interrupted the latest episode of *Dark Desires* and most recent troubles of Ramón, Tiffany, and the other residents of Forest Heights. "Thanks, baby. No, I'm good till dinner. Except for taking Barnacle for his constitutional."

"Okay. I think we'll go check out the pond. He likes barking at the frogs."

"What are we eating tonight? You're not cooking, are you?"

Mabel reminded herself Grandma was old and still in some pain. She shouldn't take offense at the wary tone of voice. "Barbecued ribs, cornbread, and beans Miss Birdie dropped off."

"Hallelujah. That Birdie's some cook."

"She sure is. We'll be back soon."

"Take your time, baby. Barnacle needs his outing."

Mabel clipped the leash on the dog, who squirmed and jumped at her feet. Barnacle should be living on a farm, she thought for the millionth time, and herding cows.

He pulled her out the door and made a beeline for the overgrown path into the woods, almost as if he had understood Mabel's conversation with Grandma. The woods at this end of the block all were park property now, but the closest few acres had originally belonged to

Helen Thornwald's family when this had been farmland. The patch of woods had grown up over most of what had once been a pasture.

The pond still survived in a grassy, weedy clearing studded with rocks, about a quarter mile back through the trees. None of this acreage had been developed, so the pond didn't appear on park maps, and few members of the public used this section of park. It almost felt like it really belonged to Grandma. As they neared the clearing, Mabel unclipped the leash.

The path connected with an overgrown dirt farm road at this point. Barnacle turned onto it and bounded ahead, aiming for his beloved pond. Regardless of weather, but especially on a hot day like this, he loved to plunge right in, barking and stampeding frogs. Barnacle, true to his cattle dog heritage, always stuck pretty close to his people which, in fact, was how he'd earned his name. And it wasn't as if there was ever anybody back here for him to bother.

Until today.

Mabel heard Barnacle's sharp barks of greeting as she stepped onto the access road. *Blast.*

"I'm so sorry, he's friendly," she babbled. "Barnacle, come."

Obviously reluctant, the joyous dog stopped jumping at the lanky younger man, who'd just emerged from the clearing, and plodded back to Mabel.

To Mabel's mortification, the guy didn't even acknowledge her apology. Head down, he stormed past her, continuing along the access road toward town. Despite his wild mass of dark hair, she saw enough of his face to realize he was scowling.

Still shaken from the sudden and uncongenial encounter, she watched him go. He took long strides and soon vanished around a bend.

Mabel frowned. He'd looked vaguely familiar, the way so many other Medicine Spring residents did to her. She just hadn't spent enough time here to recognize more than the people she saw on a regular basis.

Before releasing Barnacle again, Mabel made sure they really were alone. The clearing was quiet but for the twitter of birds and ka-chug of the bullfrogs.

"Go for it." She unclipped the dog and wandered over to the little dock to watch him plunge headlong into the pond. The water, as was typical, was scuzzy with duckweed and algae, and Barnacle resurfaced trailing slimy festoons. She was going to have to hose him off.

Sweating, Mabel fought her way through knee-high weeds to reach the dock, but immediately realized it had mostly collapsed since her last visit. She considered for a moment, then gingerly lowered herself on the edge nearest the bank. Though the boards creaked ominously, the dock held.

There had been a shabby rowboat tied up here last time. Now all that seemed to be left of that was the rope trailing off into the water.

Mabel lifted her heavy mass of hair off her neck to try to catch a breeze. It was peaceful here, and her office seemed far away. She devoutly wished she never had to go back. After almost twenty years with the firm, she was still stuck in a tiny associate's office. For the past five years, she'd also suffered the indignity of working under her law school class's "anchorman," who'd graduated dead last—and barely, at that. His father was a named partner, make of that what one would.

For a few minutes, she watched Barnacle's happy antics. Two iridescent dragonflies zipped over the water surface, landing briefly on the reeds growing along the shore. Mabel grew drowsy. The air smelled of sun-warmed grass and flowers. She was tempted to lie down on the boards for a nap, but knew she had to keep an eye on Barnacle.

Though the pond was usually fairly deep, at least toward the middle, Mabel had never seen anybody fish here. The algae and duckweed didn't seem to bother Barnacle or the frogs, but maybe fish found swimming in that water as unappealing as she did.

The level had dropped considerably with the drought. At least a foot, judging from the gap at the banks. Maybe more.

One of the dragonflies landed on a stalk sticking up from the middle of the pond. It hovered there a moment, oblivious to Barnacle's splashing.

Mabel shaded her eyes. How odd that any water plant was tall enough to stick out above the surface, midway across the pond. She'd been told the water in the middle was eight to ten feet deep, and out there where the reed stuck up had to be at least six or seven.

She squinted against the glare, wishing she'd brought sunglasses or at least her regular eyeglasses she seldom bothered to wear because the prescription gave her a headache. Even so, she could now see the dragonfly's perch wasn't the stalk of a water plant.

The stem glittered where it caught the sunlight. *Plants don't glitter like that.*

The dragonfly flitted away.

Atop the stalk that wasn't a stalk, Mabel could see a ball, a lot like the kind you'd see on a cartoon bug's antenna. Like the antennas on the Bug Man's missing van.

Chapter Eleven

Mabel might have been anxious to get home, but Barnacle clearly felt as if he'd barely started having fun. She finally convinced him to return to shore by invoking the magic word, "dinner."

All the way home, Mabel's mind raced. Was the antenna-like thing protruding from the pond surface really part of the missing Bug Man van? Should she report her suspicions to somebody? Was she reading too much into things simply because Carl Schuster's murder wouldn't do what she told it and get out of her mind?

When they arrived at the house, she started to rush inside, but then remembered how wet and filthy Barnacle was. Darn it. She clipped him to the cable by the back door and uncoiled the hose.

As soon as she'd gotten the water coming off his coat to run clear — well, mostly clear — she turned off the hose in time to watch him flop down for a good roll in the grass and dirt. Afterward, he shook mightily, sending water and bits of the back yard flying all over Mabel.

She dodged sideways. "Think you better wait out here awhile, bud."

"Mabel?"

"Coming, Grandma." Mabel slipped off her wet shoes and headed into the living room.

"Look here at this." Grandma pointed at the newspaper on her lap.

Then, she seemed to notice Mabel. "Girl, what on earth happened to you?"

"Nothing. Just Barnacle. He went swimming, and that old pond is covered in algae and duckweed, so I had to hose him off. Then, I guess you could say he hosed me off."

"Well, for heaven's sake, you just go and change. This will wait."

"No, I'm okay for now. What are you looking at?"

"It's the Bug Man's obituary. Talks about how he went to school here and came back after college to open his business. You know, I never knew his people. Birdie says they lived out past the old potato chip plant."

"Do they still live around here?"

"She says no. They moved to Florida when they retired. That's how it goes. I'm lucky my friends stayed right here like me."

"Can you save that for me to read?"

"It's not going anywhere." Grandma laid the paper on her TV tray and her glasses on top of it. "You know they say he was a coin collector. Wouldn't you think a Bug Man would be a bug collector? They put 'em in jars of something and then stick 'em to boards with labels. Always seemed kind of cruel to me, but it takes all kinds, I guess."

"It does," Mabel agreed. "Look, let me change quick, and then I'll feed Barnacle and heat up those ribs real quick, okay?"

"Do you see the remote anywhere? I'd like to watch the early news."

Mabel located the remote partway under the chair and handed it over. "I'll be back in ten."

While she was changing, Mabel called Lisa to describe what she'd found at the pond.

"I'll be right over. Just give me fifteen."

"Take forty-five. Grandma and I still need to eat, okay?"

"I guess. Maybe I should eat something too."

Mabel considered inviting Lisa to dinner but wasn't sure there was enough food in that bag from Miss Birdie to share. Especially since she herself was inordinately fond of Miss Birdie's barbecue. "Okay. See you after."

Dinner was delicious, as was anything Miss Birdie's magical fingers ever put together. Mabel gnawed the bones clean and licked her fingers. She and Grandma sighed in unison.

Grandma cackled. "She did it again. Don't know how she tolerates a hot oven in these temperatures."

"Me neither, but God bless her."

Mabel had cleared the table and was trying to make her way to the kitchen sink while Barnacle jumped and slobbered when Lisa arrived. "I'll wash these later," Mabel said, depositing the dishes on the counter. "You want something to drink? We can sit out on the porch swing."

Lisa caught her arm. "Maybe later. It's getting dark before long."

"Huh?"

"I want to see the antenna thing. Hurry up."

"There really isn't much to see." Nevertheless, Mabel found herself being dragged out the back door. "Wait. I need to tell Grandma where I'm going."

Mabel hadn't even told Grandma about what she'd seen. She wasn't sure why.

"Lisa and I are taking a little walk," she said, leaving it at that. She pushed Barnacle's eager snout away from the door. She certainly didn't need to bathe him a second time in one day.

The sun still rode above the treetops, but barely. "It's already dark back in here." Lisa caught the branch Mabel held back for her.

"We could've done this in the morning."

"Just keep moving." Lisa poked Mabel in the back. "This won't take that long."

The pond looked gloomy as a haunted swamp in the dying light, the wreckage of the old dock only adding to the general air of decay. Mabel pointed. "Do you see it?"

"Yup."

"*What* are you doing?" Mabel screeched as Lisa casually stripped off her T-shirt and shorts to reveal a swimsuit and headed for the disgusting green water.

"Hang on." Lisa pulled a pair of oversize goggles on before wading into the pond. All along the bank, frogs jumped in to join her.

Gradually, she reached the point where she was submerged all the way to the tops of her shoulders. A few yards ahead, the antenna rose above the water.

Lisa vanished. "Lisa!" Mabel wrung her hands. Should she go in and see if she was all right?

She considered the now-disturbed film of scum, through which a few dirty bubbles now rose. Nope. Somebody needed to remain ashore to call for help. And there was definitely no need for both of them to die of typhoid or giardia … or whatever one died of from contaminated water.

She could only hope Lisa was swimming down there below.

It seemed as if Lisa remained submerged for a very long time—too long, for someone without scuba gear. Mabel crept closer to the bank, wondering if she'd have to go in anyway. Lisa was her best friend, after all.

Suddenly the surface broke, and a swamp-like creature rose from the depths, trailing algae and duckweed. A creature wearing goggles.

Lisa struck for shore with a crawl stroke worthy of the lifeguard she'd been during high school vacations. She pulled herself out and plopped onto the dock, which was now listing toward the water.

Pulling off her goggles, Lisa laughed and gasped for air. "I'm such an idiot. I totally forgot to bring a towel."

Mabel frowned. "Surprisingly, I don't have one on me either. You're going to have to do what Barnacle does and roll in the grass and shake yourself."

Lisa shook her green hair, sending dirty water and specimens of pond vegetation flying all over Mabel.

"Hey!" Mabel jumped up. "Barnacle would be proud. Did you find anything down there?"

"It's there, all right."

"The Bug Man's van?"

Lisa grinned. "Surprisingly — as you would say, my sarcastic friend — visibility is somewhat limited under there. But it's definitely a vehicle."

"With a bug antenna." Mabel pointed.

Lisa waggled a hand. "Some other people, you know, put balls and stuff like that on their car antenna so they can find it in a crowded parking lot. There should be two antennas for a bug, shouldn't there?"

"This is too much of a coincidence. The bug van's missing, and here's a submerged vehicle with a bug antenna. The other one probably broke off when it went in." Mabel dialed her cell phone.

"911. What's your emergency?"

Chapter Twelve

Though it had been a late night, Mabel was out and about early the next morning. Having left Grandma with her morning coffee and book of crossword puzzles, she headed out to check whether the cat had finally sprung the trap.

Though the police had responded to Mabel's 911 call the night before, dusk was already settling in. While she and Lisa watched, they had taped off the area around the pond and closed off the public access road with plans to return in the morning. Mabel planned to be there too.

Some of Lisa's enthusiasm for murder investigation had clearly rubbed off on her. Chalk one up for the citizen detectives.

Her life as a single forty-something in a dead-end job had been predictable and, frankly, boring. That coming to Medicine Spring to help her grandmother recover from a hip replacement had made things dramatically more exciting was a sad commentary.

An overcast sky and light breeze kept the heat down, and she couldn't help wondering whether the long-awaited rain would decide to fall just in time to ruin people's Fourth of July plans. Not that she had any.

A gray-haired woman, built along much the same lines as Abraham Lincoln, was hanging more factory-faded patriotic bunting along the porch railing of Pete's house. It appeared "the wife," as Pete called her, had come home.

"Good morning." Mabel waved to catch her attention. "I'm Mabel Browne. Your husband has been letting me into the Gundersen house to try to catch a stray cat."

"Hello there. Yes, he told me. Pete!" she hollered. "Guess I missed a big to-do."

It didn't seem like a statement that needed a reply, and in fact, the wife was already talking again. "To be honest, I'm just as glad. People trampled that corner of our yard over there like you wouldn't believe. Pete!"

"I'm coming," he growled as he appeared through the front door onto the porch. "Mornin', Mabel. I see you met Viola."

At least now she had a name.

After a few minutes' polite conversation, Mabel had the key and a break in the chit-chat that gave her the opportunity to escape next door. It didn't take long to discover the bait had been stolen. Clearly, they needed to push it farther back in the trap and maybe use something stickier that the little beast couldn't just grab and run.

By the time she'd returned the key and headed home, she'd lost nearly an hour. Pete and Viola had caught her between them again and talked her ear off with details of Viola's trip, Pete's failure to keep things up in her absence, and various theories about the murder.

Mabel tried to hurry, but she had to admit she was a little bit out of shape. The sun had started to burn off the morning cloud cover. It wasn't even noon, but she had already started sweating.

When she got home, Grandma wanted help changing her compression hose — a true labor of Hercules. The stocking looked as if designed for a child, but somehow was intended to stretch over the ample lower limb of a well-fed senior citizen.

Till Mabel had accomplished the impossible, excused herself, and managed to keep Barnacle from following her, she feared she'd missed the car retrieval altogether.

She hurried along the footpath, swatting mosquitoes, and ducking thorny stems of multiflora roses only to blunder into lush patches of poison ivy. She had to remember to shower when she got home or she'd be itching all over.

When she emerged onto the rutted access road, she found it crowded with official vehicles—a couple of cruisers, a dark gray panel van, and a few cars. She wound her way to the clearing where a dive team in black wetsuits peeled down to the waist milled around in the tall grass at the pond's edge. Water only glistened on two of the divers' suits, so apparently the others were just suited up out of hopefulness.

A dark-red tow truck sat on the bank with its winch extended out over the pond. A pale-green van hung suspended as water streamed from its wheel wells and broken windows.

As she studied it, Mabel could make out the faint script in a darker green reading, "The Bug Man" on the van's dented side panel. The lighter green color was algae, she now realized. The human-sized dead bug that Grandma's friends had described as being mounted on the roof was no longer attached, and only one crooked antenna remained affixed above the windshield.

A uniformed male cop approached her, both hands raised in a pushing gesture. "Ma'am, you're going to have to leave the area. Did you not see the barricade?"

"No," Mabel said honestly, craning her neck around the officer for a better view. "I came on the path through the woods, and there was no barricade at all."

"Well, it's time for you to head back the way you came. This is a crime scene." He waved an arm at the yellow tape. "It's also very dangerous for civilians."

Mabel took a reluctant backward step. "I found the van last evening. My name's Mabel Browne. I called it in."

"Thank you, Ms. Browne, we appreciate that. Do we have your address? We'll be around to talk to you a little bit later, but now you need to clear the area."

He made another shooing gesture, as if he were driving off an annoying animal.

Mabel backed away slowly, but as soon as the officer had turned around, she raised her cell phone and snapped a few pictures to show Grandma and Lisa. As she did, the phone rang.

"Mabel. Lisa. I've got a theory."

"That's great. I'm just leaving the pond. They brought the van up."

"Darn it. I knew I should've cancelled my dentist appointment. What did it look like?"

"Banged up, covered in algae. I took a few pictures."

"Stay there. I'm on my way over now."

"You're going to need to come to Grandma's. We aren't welcome at the pond."

Lisa sniffed. "A lot of thanks we get for our efforts. Did you check on your cat?"

"Yeah. She stole the bait again."

"Smart kitty. Sounds like she's doing okay, though. Maybe you ought to just give up."

Mabel's own strong reaction surprised her. "I can't do that. What if her wound gets infected or—"

Lisa snorted.

"I mean she keeps going in and out of that house. A coyote could get her, or she might get hit by a car."

Lisa laughed. "You got yourself attached to the feisty little thing. No shame in that."

***

When Lisa arrived at the house, Mabel was attempting to work off some of Barnacle's excess energy by flinging a ball for him to chase. The blare of Grandma's baseball game came through the open window. She was a devoted lifelong fan of the Pittsburgh Pirates. This currently meant a lot of groaning and yelling were going on.

"Let's sit on the porch." Mabel grabbed the slimy ball Barnacle thrust against her leg. "You want a drink?"

"No, thanks. I'm good."

Mabel led the way to the front porch with Barnacle leaping up at her as she held the ball above her head. Once they'd climbed the steps, she opened the front door and tossed the ball inside. The dog bounded down the hall after it, and she shut the door behind him.

A moment later, sounds of snuffling, scratching, and whining came from inside. At a sharp command from Grandma, the noises stopped.

"Meanie." Lisa shook her head in mock reproach.

"I already played with that perpetual motion machine for half an hour in this heat. Grandma will give him a cracker from her stash, and he'll be snoozing on her feet in about two minutes. Let's go back here."

Lisa followed Mabel to the far side of the house where the covered porch wrapped around to face the dense trees of the park. Leafy shadows cast by the arching maple branches bobbed gently in a breeze. "Ooh, nice and shady. Feels good."

Mabel plugged in the fan that had been squirreled away behind one of the big old wicker chairs. As the air began to stir, she lifted the heavy mass of hair off her neck. "Much better."

"Are these safe to sit on?" Lisa poked at the splintering chair arm.

"If they hold me, they'll definitely hold you." Mabel eyed her diminutive friend. It was hard not to envy her a bit, but not enough to induce Mabel to give up French fries and dessert.

Lisa pressed a hand against the chair seat before cautiously lowering her bottom. "Quick. Show me the pictures of the van, and then I'll tell you my brainstorm."

After a few minutes of questions and exclamations, she handed Mabel's phone back to her. "Did the police say when they were coming by?"

"No, but it might be any time, so tell me your idea before we get interrupted."

"Okay, here goes. I'm thinking the pest control guys had a home burglary racket going on, right?"

"Whoa—hold up. Where'd you get a crazy idea like that?" Mabel asked.

Lisa sniffed. "You told me about it, remember?"

"No, I didn't. I may have mentioned Ms. Katherine Ann had a very complicated theory that involved something along those lines. But it involved fleas and didn't make any sense."

Lisa leaned forward. "Oh, but it does make sense. That is, I don't know what else your grandma's friend thought was going on, but how about this? The bug guys are getting all this access to people's houses, okay? And they're getting the perfect opportunity to go through all this expensive stuff while there's nobody home because the homeowners have to leave while the place is getting bombed."

Mabel waved a hand in front of Lisa's face. "Not happening. Once the cloud of poison gas clears, people are coming back. Don't you think they might notice their computers and jewelry are suddenly missing? It's not going to take Hercule Poirot. Even your kindergarteners could figure that out."

"I didn't say the bug guys were going to clear the house out on the spot. They'd probably wait awhile, then come back after enough time had gone by that nobody would make the connection."

"If they're using a copy of the house keys, I'd think that would point right at them."

"So they don't use a key. They do an actual break-in. They'd know which houses didn't have alarms, didn't have dogs. They could chat people up while they're setting up the job and get a feel for whether people are normally home during the day."

"Maybe. So Carl Schuster's murdered in an empty house ... why?"

"From what Hernandez already told us, he and Schuster weren't on the best terms to begin with. Say the bug guys were fighting over the loot. They might even have been using the house to stash it. Or maybe Schuster wanted out and was threatening to go to the police."

Mabel thought for a moment. "From what Ms. Katherine Ann said, people suspected them at the time. But when you come right down to it, we can't even prove the bug guys had anything to do with those break-ins. How are we going to know where the burglaries happened? And whether they had any pest work done?"

"*The Statesman* police blotter should get us pretty close. They may even have run an article if there was an obvious rash of burglaries."

"That still won't tell us if any of them hired the Bug Man."

"But his partner Hernandez will. We'll ask."

What Mabel intended to say never left her mouth because, at that moment, she heard the crunch of tires in the side driveway. Barnacle immediately began barking and throwing himself at the back door.

Lisa jumped up. "Oh, darn. I've got a student coming for tutoring in half an hour, and I'm going to be blocked in."

Mabel followed Lisa to the front steps. A police SUV sat in the driveway, and a young male officer was emerging from the driver's seat.

Mabel watched Lisa explain, get rewarded by a broad smile from the stocky, red-faced young cop, and wave brightly at Mabel before getting into her car. "Call me," Lisa mouthed. Even in her late forties, she looked years younger, and she had always had that knack of charming males of all ages. A knack Mabel had never and would never have.

After Lisa had departed with a merry toot, and the policeman had parked once again, Mabel stepped down to greet him. "Mabel Browne?"

"Yes, sir. You're here about the bug van?"

"You have a moment to talk?"

"I do, if you could just give me a moment to check on my grandmother? She had a recent hip replacement, and I need to let her know what's going on real quick."

"Not a problem."

Mabel showed him to a seat on the porch before stepping inside to explain about the police. Barnacle, of course, nearly bowled her over in his eagerness to get outside and inspect the visitor, and she finally had to have Grandma hold his collar.

"I'm fine, baby, if you could just grab me an icepack and that new bag of cheddar-sour cream chips. And make sure you fill me in later."

Mabel raised her eyebrows. She knew Grandma couldn't be trusted with a full chip bag, especially considering her cholesterol. But it was really hard to boss one's grandmother. Plus the cop was waiting.

"Okay, Grandma. I'll give you a full report later on over dinner."

Leaving Grandma and Barnacle sharing the cheddar-sour cream chips—after sampling a handful herself for quality-control purposes—Mabel returned to the porch. The officer sat waiting on the porch swing, looking at his phone.

"Can I get you a drink?"

"No, thank you, ma'am. Just have a few questions for you, and then we'll need you to come in and sign a statement for us."

Mabel sat in the old aluminum lawn chair and felt the yellow plastic seat strips sink beneath her weight. It seemed to her the frame spread a bit too. *It's just an old chair,* she reassured herself.

The officer glanced at his phone again. "This won't take too long. I'm sure you'll want to eat dinner soon."

True to his word, he walked Mabel through her discovery of the bug van quite efficiently. Only pausing to observe how "unusual" it was that she'd been the one to discover both the body and the missing van—and all in the space of a few days.

Mabel gave him a sharp glance. Lisa had warned her that police always took a hard look at the person who first reported the body. Apparently, she had gleaned this info from one of her true crime podcasts. Was she a suspect?

The cop was writing himself a note and didn't look up. Mabel clamped her lips together. One thing she'd learned from her years as an attorney—however humble—was to keep her mouth shut if she wasn't being asked a direct question.

"Can you tell me about the individual you reported seeing on the road to the pond that evening? Describe him, if you can, and the encounter."

Mabel pulled her thoughts back from her potential jeopardy and shut her eyes as she tried to recall what he'd referred to as "the encounter." "Well … he was on the skinny side. And pretty tall." Mabel stood and raised one hand above her head to the approximate height.

"Over six feet, then?"

"Definitely. Though some of that was hair … he had a lot of hair."

"Color?"

"White. I mean he was White. His hair was dark. I can't really describe him—it was shady under the trees, and we didn't really talk. Just passed by each other."

"You didn't know him?"

She shook her head.

"Was that unusual, running into someone back there?"

"A little bit. Not a lot of people go there, but I do run into people trying to fish sometimes. Or just walking, maybe with off-leash dogs. Kids messing around."

"Anything else you're aware of? Drugs? Underage drinking? Maybe, um, lovers' lane activity?"

Mabel's head jerked up. It had never occurred to her that she might run into people back by the pond who didn't want to be observed. "No."

The policeman asked several more questions, but Mabel had little to offer. When he'd finally concluded the interview and thanked her, she headed back inside.

Something gnawed at the back of her mind, but she couldn't quite get a handle on it. Mabel set the oven on medium low and put the aluminum pans of leftover ribs, cornbread, and beans in to heat. She worked automatically, dodging around Barnacle's eager interference as he sniffed the air.

"Dinner in about a half hour," she told Grandma, handing her the newspaper she'd collected from the delivery box. "I need to look something up online while the ribs heat, okay?"

Grandma nodded. Dad had called to check in, and he and Grandma were having a conversation over the blare of the TV. Luckily, he didn't share Mom's ongoing need to lecture Mabel about her life choices, such as second-story kitten rescues culminating in homicide investigations. Mabel's ear was still ringing from her most recent attack of maternal advice.

The guest room bed had been Mabel's ever since childhood visits. Other than the unsettling view of the Sauer ax murder house, it was cozy and comforting. The old floorboards creaked, the oak furniture was dinged, and the bedsprings sagged, but the room always felt like a hug. Grandma had made those white curtains, and she'd woven the rug and pieced the faded quilt of remnants cut from worn clothing.

Mabel settled herself on the bed. As she'd always done, she smoothed out the blue-flowered quilt patch that had been cut from her favorite second-grade dress. She'd had her school picture taken in that dress before she ruined it forever by throwing up grape juice all down the front.

She opened her laptop and searched the local TV news site for the footage from the afternoon of her discovery of Carl Schuster's body. Mostly, the camera focused on the field reporter with occasional pans of the house or the crowd. When someone gave an interview, they got their moment on camera too.

Briefly, Mabel saw herself scuttling away from the microphone. "I look like a chimney sweep," she muttered, "except who ever saw a chimney that wide?" Silently vowing to go on a diet—soon—she watched as the camera panned the crowd. There was that young man, who'd talked to Mabel at the scene, scrolling on his phone toward the back of the crowd.

She paused the video, but realized she'd failed to catch the fleeting image. After fiddling a moment, she got back to the right frame. Mabel squinted, then turned and fumbled on the nightstand for her glasses.

Yes, she decided after studying the blurry image, he could definitely be the same man she'd seen out on the pond road. That guy hadn't looked up at her, but he was tall enough, and he had the same bushy hair.

Which proved exactly nothing. Mabel sighed. She had been in both places the same time he had. It was a small town, and coincidences happened. And after all, it wasn't as if something had just happened at the pond. The van had been missing—and probably in the water—for months at that point.

Should she mention it to the police? Yeah, she should probably mention it to the police. More importantly, Grandma had seemed to recognize the guy. But could she remember who he was?

Chapter Thirteen

A dark nose thrust through the crack in the door, and Barnacle bounded in. He put his front paws up on the bed and grinned at Mabel.

"Oh, do you smell the ribs?"

As soon as she stepped into the hallway, the delectable scent of Miss Birdie's home cooking put an extra bounce in Mabel's step. Solving crimes certainly gave one an appetite.

Before she'd made it to the bend in the stairway, her cellphone rang. When she saw the caller ID, Mabel groaned inwardly. She hesitated, thumb poised to mute the ringer.

No, she couldn't do that. Though highly unlikely, it might be important. Plus, he'd only leave a message, and then she'd have to call him back.

"Mabel!" Grandma's voice drifted upward. "I think dinner's done."

"I'll be right down, Grandma. I have to take a quick call."

She sat on the step, trying to ignore Barnacle's whines and small yelps.

"Hello?"

"Mabel." The too-loud male voice made her clench her teeth. Even Mom's well-intentioned counsel would have been infinitely better than this.

"Todd here. We need to start prepping Jameson for trial, and you seem to have misplaced several files. One, Meredith's deposition. Two, that box of documents from the McCandless branch office. Three—"

"All in the vacant paralegal office in the back corner of the litigation section. As I told you in the memo I gave you before I left."

"I never received such a memo."

Mabel released the breath she'd been unconsciously holding. Conversations with her former law school classmate—now managing partner of the firm—tended to cause her respiratory system to shut down, as if she were entering a toxic cloud.

"I placed it in your hand, Todd. You know—never mind. My grandmother needs me. I'll just resend it to you by email."

"Wait. I need to ask you about—"

"I really have to go now. Why not drop me an email, and I'll see if I can help."

"I'm under a great deal of time pressure here, Mabel, which you do not seem to appreciate. I have a complex case going to trial in ten days, and your departure comes at a very inopportune time."

"Look. Sounds like you need to get to work. And I do need to tend to my grandmother. Who's had recent major surgery. I left everything in order for you. Good chat."

Mabel hung up, knowing she was playing with fire. Todd could be vindictive. But it was hard having to treat someone who'd scraped through law school, riding on her coattails, as if he were the return of Justice Oliver Wendell Holmes.

She dismissed him from her mind and headed for the kitchen. As she passed the living room, she stuck her head in to see Grandma. "Do you want to eat in the kitchen?"

Grandma folded the evening paper and laid it on her TV tray. "Goodness, yes. I'm so tired of this room. I sit here all day, eat here, and sleep all night in here too. Hand me my walker, would you, baby? I need to make a stop."

Mabel helped Grandma onto her feet and aimed her toward the hallway. She was glad her father had insisted on installing a tiny second bathroom a couple years ago. She could never have managed to care for Grandma at home, otherwise.

As they ate their dinner a bit later, Mabel shared the details of the raising of the van. Grandma paused her steady work through the plateful of ribs, beans, and cornbread, to exclaim periodically. "I can't believe it, baby. This is the most excitement we've seen around here in over seventy years."

Mabel knew she was referring to the Sauer ax murders, which had occurred just yards away when Grandma was ten, and never been solved. She unfolded the paper again to the photo from the day of the discovery of the body and passed it to Grandma.

"Have you remembered who this guy right here is? You said before he looked kind of familiar."

Grandma dropped the rib she'd been gnawing on and wiped her hands. They were so messy with barbecue sauce it looked as if she'd perpetrated the Sauer killings herself. She frowned over the photo. "I've tried to bring it back, but I can't."

As Mabel's face fell, Grandma smiled. "I'll tell you what. I can call the girls. I'll bet one of them knows. They'll be anxious to hear the whole story about the van. And I'll promise them cupcakes."

"We don't have any cupcakes."

"Oh, we will, baby. You're going to bake them."

Mabel drew back and raised her hands in protest. "I don't bake, remember?"

"Honey, I laid in a supply of mix before my operation. You'll find it in the cabinet over the fridge."

"Is the frosting in the mix too?"

Grandma laughed. "Comes in a can. Same place. Now if you can just stretch the phone cord over this way …"

Mabel pulled the heavy, old, black Bakelite phone toward her. When it was time for her to go back home and leave Grandma alone, they would have to convince her to replace it with a cordless variety. The burner phone Mabel had brought for her convalescence refused to hold a charge, and Grandma would never plug it in.

"Thanks. Now get cracking."

While Mabel readied the dishes for washing, and started mixing chocolate cupcake batter, she heard Grandma chatting with Miss Birdie and Ms. Katherine Ann. Clearly audible girlish squeals erupted on the other end of the line as Grandma teased the raising of the bug van from the watery depths.

Mabel scooted her own phone closer and texted Lisa.

Want to come for cupcakes? And detecting?

Her phone pinged almost immediately.

On my way.

Lisa arrived first, and it was a good thing. She made the pot of tea and gathered cups, plates, and silverware. Though the chocolate fudge mix produced a dozen cupcakes almost magically, Mabel had forgotten to use the frilled cupcake papers. And when she tried to frost them, the topping began melting like an ice cream cone in the summer sun.

"Here." Lisa shooed Mabel aside and found spots in the fridge to chill both cupcakes and frosting. "First of all," she told Mabel, "you can't mess with frosting till you get those babies out of the pan. I hope you greased it first."

Mabel thought. "Yeah, I think so. I mean I did."

"Good. They need to cool a bit, and then we'll loosen them with a table knife."

Barnacle had been trailing around the kitchen, sniffing the air. Now, he gave up and plodded, head down, to lie at Grandma's feet. He seemed disappointed by Mabel's lack of generosity in licking the beaters herself.

As Lisa bustled around, washing the baking things and tidying the kitchen, Mabel filled her in on the plan to try to identify the strange man who'd appeared both at the crime scene and later at the pond. "Grandma's memory isn't what it was, but she thinks one of the others ought to be able to remember the name that she can't quite bring up."

"Cool. One more loose end to clear up, anyway. Are you planning on setting the cat trap again this evening?"

"Yeah, I have to. You can come too if you want."

By the time Miss Birdie and Ms. Katherine Ann arrived, Lisa had managed to remove nine of the cupcakes in reasonably good condition and had them frosted and plated. Barnacle came running to jump and bark at the back door, so Mabel held him back as Lisa served as greeter.

"My, your kitchen smells good." Ms. Katherine Ann sniffed the air appreciatively.

"Come on in here, girls. Mabel, fetch those cupcakes, baby." Grandma's voice boomed from the front room.

Miss Birdie, attired in one of the flowered dresses she favored when not suited up for a power walk, greeted Grandma with a peck on the cheek. She sat on the end of the hospital bed. Ms. Katherine Ann followed her, looking cool in a floral T-shirt and hot pink Bermudas that revealed shapely if vein-patterned legs. Miss Birdie scootched over.

"So what's the story with the bug van?" Ms. Katherine Ann sank onto the mattress and accepted tea and a cupcake. As she did, the other end of the mattress rose noticeably, and Miss Birdie's feet left the floor.

"Tell 'em, Mabel honey." Grandma licked frosting off her fingers.

Mabel repeated her account of the raising of the van to the accompaniment of exclamations worthy of the watery resurrection of Confederate submarine H. L. Hunley. Lisa, having heard it all before, continued passing cupcakes and pouring tea.

After Mabel's story ended, she took questions for a couple minutes before Grandma cut in. "Now here's the thing, girls. You know Mabel ran into this fella over at the crime scene, and she thinks she saw him again later, near the pond, not long before she found the van. There's a picture in the paper she thinks is the same guy. He looks kind of familiar, but I'll be darned if I can remember."

"Give us a try." Ms. Katherine Ann waggled her chocolatey fingers.

"Lisa dear, would you please pass Katherine another napkin?" Grandma asked. "Mabel, hand this to Birdie, please."

Mabel folded the paper to display the photo and pointed as she placed it in Miss Birdie's clean hands. "This guy right here. Do either of you remember seeing him that day? Or know who he is?"

The two old ladies hovered over the paper. "I do remember seeing this guy." Ms. Katherine Ann poked a finger at the photo, leaving a chocolate spot. "Or at least, his hair. I didn't really pay much attention to him."

Miss Birdie closed her eyes. "You know who he looks like? Imagine him heavier with glasses and starting to lose his hair."

Ms. Katherine Ann squinted. "His hair's all I noticed."

"You're right," Grandma said. "Now I remember. Jack Armbruster!"

Miss Birdie smiled. "That's it."

"Well, this guy looks way too young to be Jack," Ms. Katherine Ann said. "And there's no way he grew his hair back. 'Less he was wearing a wig. You think that's a wig?"

"Goodness' sake, Katherine." Grandma rolled her eyes. "I don't think it's a wig. I think it's Jack's son, what's-his-name."

"Who's Jack Armbruster?" Mabel asked.

"He lived in that house where you found the body." All three ladies answered at the same time, in some variation of the same words.

Lisa frowned. "I thought it was Gundersens."

Miss Birdie nodded. "Before them. Armbrusters moved out of that place probably twenty-some years ago to a new house in that plan where they tore down the dog food plant. Husband worked as a home health aide and she was a waitress. Now, I can't say I'm 100% sure it's the boy. I'm thinking there was a son, but heavens. He would've left here when he graduated from high school and went off to college about ten-fifteen years back."

"Folks retired to Florida," Ms. Katherine Ann said. "They're long gone too."

Mabel removed Barnacle's paw from her knee and slipped him a piece of cupcake. "Why would this guy be in town, do you think?"

Grandma shook her head. "Who knows? Wasn't there just a high school reunion a while back? He'd be about right for a ten-or-fifteen-year."

"Maybe he came back, and it made him homesick for Medicine Spring," Ms. Katherine Ann suggested, "and he stuck around awhile."

"Three months? That would've been back in the spring," Grandma said. "Surely he's got to be working somewhere, even with that hair." She shook her head.

Mabel moved Barnacle's steamy snout from her lap. Giving him a piece of cupcake had been a rookie mistake.

"Maybe he moved back. He does look like Jack, back in the old days." Miss Birdie pondered, turning her teacup this way and that in her hands. "You know who else would have been about the same age as this kid right now? Mabel's body."

"Oh, maybe so." Grandma rooted around for the obituary. "Yeah, here it is. Do either of you recall his people? I wonder if they were churchgoers. They didn't belong to ours."

The other women shook their heads. "No," Ms. Katherine Ann said. "Can't say I ever met them. Anybody out that way went to the other elementary school too."

"Was the dead boy about the same age as Jack's son?" Miss Birdie asked.

"If we're saying ten or fifteen years out of high school, then yes."

"Maybe they knew each other in high school," Ms. Katherine Ann mused. "Maybe the Bug Man gave Jack's kid one of those slushies, and Jack's boy came back for revenge."

For a moment, everyone stared at her. Then, Lisa's eyes brightened. "Oh. She means a swirly."

Grandma shook her head.

"Katherine." Miss Birdie's voice was patient. "Nobody's going to return after a decade to kill someone as revenge for getting their head shoved in a toilet."

"A public high school restroom, Birdie? A *boys'* room?" Ms. Katherine Ann shuddered. "I'd wake up screaming every night for the rest of my life."

Mabel nudged Lisa's foot with hers and tipped her head toward the door. "Excuse us, but we need to get that cat trap set up while we can still see in there." She got up, and Lisa followed suit.

"Do you need anything before we go?" Lisa asked.

"Katherine and I can take care of anything Big Mabel needs before we leave, girls, thank you." Miss Birdie squeezed Mabel's and Lisa's hands.

Barnacle started to follow, but Mabel nudged him back. Looking discouraged, he flopped himself down on Grandma's feet.

***

Nearly an hour had passed by the time they'd finally gotten the trap set. When Lisa dropped Mabel back at Grandma's, Ms. Katherine Ann's yacht-sized red car was gone.

"I'm off tomorrow," Lisa said. "So why don't I pick you up about 9:30, and we can go check out these burglaries?"

Mabel couldn't prevent herself from heaving a deep sigh. "Seriously? Don't you have anything better to do with your day off?" The way Lisa complained about her part-time summer job as a grocery cashier, one would certainly think so.

Lisa just laughed. "Hope you catch your kitty."

Mabel sighed again. "Me too. I mean I'm sure she must be okay. Unless her cut got infected. But she shouldn't be running around loose. That's how cats get run over or eaten by owls."

"I hope you're not planning on keeping her. She sounds feral to me. And most of those feral cats never do adjust normally to being house pets."

"Of course not. I just want to get her to safety. Maybe take her to the humane society."

Even as she said it, Mabel felt a twinge of doubt. Once she went back to her small townhouse rental, away from Grandma and Lisa, life was going to get pretty lonely. She'd gotten used to that life—work long hours, come home to a frozen dinner, and crash on the couch. But after spending time here for a while, Mabel had to admit she was less than anxious to go back. *Did* she want to keep the little cat?

Chapter Fourteen

Mabel's heart sank that morning when she checked her cat trap. For the first time since she'd been setting it, the bait hadn't been stolen. The bad news was that it was untouched.

"If she's okay, she'd be eating. She knows there's been food here every night."

Lisa shrugged. "Maybe somebody took her in."

Mabel stared at her. "You're kidding, right? How's someone going to 'take her in,' if she won't let anybody near her? You notice I haven't had any luck. I'm afraid something's happened to her."

Lisa jostled her arm. "Well, don't worry about it now. We'll retool your trap tonight. I'm sure she's fine."

Mabel was not reassured. "She's really small, and I still think she's hurt. Maybe a coyote got her."

"There's nothing we can do about it at this point. Let's check next door. Maybe they've seen her."

Reluctantly, Mabel followed Lisa to the stairs. "I'll just leave the bait where it is, in case she sneaks back in during the day."

When they rang the bell next door, Pete's wife answered.

"It was around here yesterday afternoon," she told them. "I had to chase it away from my bird bath." Viola folded her arms across her chest. "I hope you catch it soon. Otherwise, I'm going to have to call Animal Control. We need to get the place closed up before Phil and Marge Gundersen get home too. They're freaking out over this body."

As they trudged back to Lisa's car, Mabel scanned the bushes and along the street. No glimpse of black-and-gold fur.

"Since we're already out, you want to go check a few places that were burglarized?" Lisa clicked the remote to unlock her doors.

"Okay. But how do we even know which those are? All the police blotter gave us was a street name."

"Ah, but Butternut Way only has six houses. We can just start there."

"All right." Mabel slid into the passenger seat. "We'll say we heard they used an exterminator recently, and we're looking for a review. Then, if they used the Bug Man, we'll bring up the reported burglaries and say we're concerned they might be involved."

"It's a plan."

"But keep your eye peeled for Koi," Mabel added.

"What?"

"The cat."

"It sounded as if you said koi. I thought you might be looking for fishponds, for some bizarre reason."

Mabel squirmed and looked out the window. "I just kind of think of her like that. With her long whiskers and those colors, she just looks like a fancy little goldfish."

"I think you're mixing like three different types of fish, but that's kind of sweet. You really care about her, don't you?"

"Well, yeah. I sure don't want Viola calling Animal Control on her."

Lisa patted Mabel's hand and started the engine. "We'll get her. Just you wait and see."

***

Half an hour later, they had struck out again. Although they'd managed to locate a house on Butternut that had used the Bug Man's services, the home hadn't been burglarized. The woman who'd answered the door pointed out a blue house two doors down, which had been broken into, but she couldn't say whether they'd recently hired an exterminator. Nobody was home there anyway.

Lisa was undeterred. In fact, she was quite pumped up. "There's your nexus, Mabes. Two houses in the same block, and the burglary happened a week after the Bug Man was over there."

Mabel shook her head. One house with bugs. Another house with a break-in. She could see nothing more than a minor coincidence.

They'd gotten a late start that morning and were already well into the afternoon. Grandma had assured her she was doing fine and said Ms. Katherine Ann had brought pizza for their lunch. But Mabel's breakfast felt eons ago, and her stomach grumbled about it.

Before Lisa could come up with another line of investigation, Mabel spoke up. "I'm probably half an hour from dying of starvation over here. Can we please just eat now?"

Lisa checked her phone. "Oh, all right. How about Old Tom's?"

"Sure." Old Tom's was a fish place along Cloud Lake, named for a legendary giant fish supposedly spotted numerous times over the past hundred years, but never caught.

As Lisa drove, Mabel kept watch out her window. At one point, she was almost sure she saw Koi dart into the shrubberies by the elementary school. "Stop, stop."

Though Lisa obediently pulled over, and Mabel poked around the bushes for several minutes, they saw no further sign of the little cat. "That's good news, though, isn't it? At least, you know now she's okay."

"Not really. It was just a quick glimpse. I'm not even sure it was her."

Still, Mabel felt a small boost of encouragement. Somehow, this in turn, made her hungrier.

Ten minutes later, Lisa turned down the dirt road leading to the public boat docks and Old Tom's Restaurant. Woods golden with sunlight crowded both sides of the narrow road.

When they emerged into the unpaved parking area, they found it nearly deserted. "Middle of a weekday afternoon," Lisa said. "Lunch is over, too early for dinner."

Their feet crunched over the gravel as they crossed to the broad wooden steps leading up to the enclosed dining area. Mabel took a deep breath of the fresh air, laden with a fishy fragrance combined with a hint of French fries. The aroma instantly transported her back to childhood days fishing at the lake with her grandpa, followed by lunch at Old Tom's.

Out on the water sat a rowboat occupied by a man in a bucket hat, and a small boy, fishing poles in hand. Mabel smiled. She asked for a table on the deck, and she and Lisa both ordered fish sandwich platters, Lisa's with a glass of water, and Mabel's with a large Coke.

Lisa frowned. "All that sugar's bad for you."

"I need the sugar and caffeine for energy," Mabel insisted. "Besides, I'm eating healthy. I'm having fish."

"The fish is fried, plus it comes with … Oh, never mind."

Both their phones vibrated almost simultaneously. "Hi ..." Lisa's voice went all soft the way it always did when she talked to her boyfriend Tim. She excused herself and walked over to the railing to talk.

Mabel rolled her eyes when she saw her own caller ID and silenced the ringer. *Todd again. Let him leave a message.* It was going to be painful when her vacation ended, and she had to go back to the office. She was thoroughly sick of being the wind beneath Todd's wings.

The waitress set down their drinks. Mabel took a big, appreciative gulp. She studied Lisa, leaning over the railing and looking out across the lake as she chatted on the phone. If Mabel started drinking water and taking half her meal to go, would she be tiny and slim, and have a nice boyfriend too?

Nope. Mabel was a solid 5'9" in flip flops and, as her pediatrician had told Mom years ago, "big-boned." And as for boyfriends, she'd long ago learned her somewhat blunt personality did not exactly attract men.

Lisa returned to the table at the same time their food arrived. For the next half hour, they discussed how to improve Mabel's odds of trapping the elusive Koi. While Mabel ate her sandwich and fries, Lisa nibbled at her food and scrolled how-to articles online.

"Okay," she finally announced. "I think I know what to do, but we'll need to stop at a hardware store on our way back to the house."

"And the grocery store," Mabel said. "I want to pick up some liverwurst. Cheese just doesn't seem to be her thing." She counted out money for her check. "Oh. I nearly forgot. Grandma also wanted me to pick up two books they've been holding for her at the library."

"That's great. If we scoot over there, it'll take us right past another pretty short block where a burglary happened early in the spring."

Mabel felt torn. She was tired of ringing doorbells and dodging agitated dogs. Especially when the homeowners made her feel as welcome as a guy wanting to give you an estimate on new windows or tell you why you should vote for his cousin running for sheriff.

Plus, her newly awakened instincts as a citizen detective told her they were missing something. She sighed.

Lisa couldn't have missed hearing the sigh, but she started the car as if Mabel hadn't made a sound. "This'll only take a couple minutes."

***

The old stone house sat behind a matching wall covered in ivy. Lisa parked at the curb. "Come on, Mabel. You're my back-up."

"What do you mean, 'back-up'? You don't need me. What am I supposed to do … keep my gun drawn?"

"Haha." Lisa tugged Mabel's arm. "You'll notice things I don't. Or remember what I forget to ask."

Grumbling under her breath, Mabel trailed Lisa through the gate and up to the front door. Painted dark red, it sported a patriotic wreath featuring tiny American flags, red silk roses, and ribbon printed with stars. While Lisa rang the bell, Mabel situated herself a few paces back, admiring the well-groomed grass and shrubs.

She pondered her escape in the event a guard dog burst through the door. She could possibly make it to the car, but without a key, her best bet would be to jump on the hood. The unlikelihood of her sticking that landing was concerning.

To Mabel's relief, she heard no barking as the peal of the doorbell reverberated through the house. A moment later, the door eased open a few cautious inches.

"Hi, ma'am. Sorry to bother you. I hope you don't mind — your address was given to me as having had work done by the Bug Man extermination company? I've been looking for recommendations for an ant infestation."

The door opened a bit wider, to reveal a small, white-haired woman neatly attired in navy slacks and a white tunic. Her name, according to a small brass plate on the door, appeared to be Woodlawn. "Yes. I used their services. They did well enough, but I believe the man who actually did the work is now deceased."

"Yes, ma'am. I understand that. But overall, you'd recommend the company?"

The lady hesitated. "Their prices seemed a bit high, but they don't have a lot of competition in this immediate area, unfortunately."

Her restless fingers went to the base of her throat and she inclined her head closer to Lisa. "I'm probably being very silly, but I did feel a bit uneasy ..."

Mabel had been surreptitiously checking the phone in her pocket. She looked up.

"The man who was here ..."

"Carl Schuster." Mabel stepped nearer.

"Yes, was that the name of the man they found dead?"

Mabel nodded, hoping Lisa wouldn't open her mouth and identify Mabel as the person who'd found him.

"He made me ... uncomfortable. I saw him looking at my things, and I just didn't like being alone in the house with him. Then, not even two weeks later, I had the burglary."

"Oh, no." Lisa tilted her head in a listening attitude.

"Yes. I'm sure it was coincidental, but the thought did cross my mind …"

"I hope you didn't lose anything precious," Mabel said.

"I did, though. Someone took all my jewelry and a silver picture frame that sat on my end table. It had portraits of my late husband and son in it. At least most of the jewelry wasn't expensive. But I wish he hadn't taken the one piece my husband gave me when we were first married, when he was a poor graduate student. It was a beautiful bracelet, and it brought back such happy memories."

Her eyes misted. "Whoever stole it probably ended up just tossing it in the weeds somewhere."

"I'm so sorry," Lisa said. "Was that all you lost?"

"He took a camera, a few coin books my son had collected while he was growing up. And my wedding silver." The woman dug a tissue from her pants pocket and dabbed at her eyes. "I wasn't here when the break-in occurred. I was at my garden club. But I can barely sleep at night now, thinking whoever did it might come back."

Unless, Mabel thought, he had already died in the Gundersen house as the woman had suggested. "Did you report your suspicions?"

She shook her head. "Oh, I guess I did mention that man had been in my house, but I had no real evidence against him. I suppose he was cleared. And it wasn't as if anything disappeared while he was working here. Whoever did it broke a window to get in."

Mabel glanced toward the stone wall that separated the front yard from the street. She was sure she'd seen a sign for a security company posted by the gate. Surely, an alarm would've immediately sounded.

Mrs. Woodlawn seemed to notice the look. "I had the security system put in since the break-in."

"I hope they find out who did this," Lisa said.

"And that you're able to get your things back," Mabel added.

As they returned to Lisa's car, Mabel thought Lisa's pet theory might very well be correct. There was at least some glimmer of evidence pointing toward Schuster as the serial burglar working the area. A dispute between him and his business partner — and partner in crime? — could easily have ended in homicide. Or perhaps even an enraged homeowner/burglary victim could've tracked him to the Gundersen house.

"But why the Gundersen house?" Mabel asked, thinking out loud.

"What?" Lisa paused with the key in the ignition.

"Okay. I'm beginning to think you're onto something with the burglaries. But what brought him to that empty house?"

Lisa started the car. "Like I said before. Maybe he was stashing the loot in the house, since he knew it was vacant. Or he and his partner — Hernandez or someone else."

Mabel shook her head in a vain attempt to settle her thoughts into a coherent pattern. "Well, what now?"

"We need to stop at the hardware before it closes. And you wanted to hit the grocery."

"All right. Hardware first since it closes the earliest. Then, I think, library next, to pick up Grandma's books because she also wanted a half gallon of ice cream, and that won't keep. So after the library, we'll stop at the store for bait and the ice cream, run Grandma's stuff to her, then go set the trap."

"Sounds like a plan, but you better call Pete and make sure he'll be around to let us into the house."

"It's their bowling night. He promised to leave the key for me, so we can go any time."

The wind was kicking up, tossing the treetops and driving gray clouds across the sky. Mabel hoped the weather held off till she could finally get her trap reset.

Chapter Fifteen

The library lot was mostly empty by the time Lisa finally pulled into a spot. "You go on ahead in. I'm just going to wait out here and check my messages," she said.

The Bartles Grove Community Library occupied a 1926 former school building, two stories of red brick with tall, skinny windows glinting in the late-afternoon sun. A grant had financed the ground-level, handicap-accessible entrance years ago. Still, Mabel climbed the broad central steps to the main floor by habit as she'd done since childhood.

The checkout desk faced the door. *Drat.* Grandma's friend, the too-talkative Thelma Neuhaus, whom she'd met at the crime scene, was the volunteer on duty.

Thelma's round red cheeks broadened in a smile. "Why, Mabel. Good to see you. I was just about to call your grandma again about her pickup."

Mabel returned the smile. "No need."

Instead of locating the books, Thelma leaned closer, resting her expansive bosom on the counter. "Say, I didn't realize when we talked the other day that the body you found was Carl Schuster."

Mabel opened her mouth to say she hadn't either, but Thelma continued talking. "I *know* him." She stared at Mabel with big eyes rimmed with spiderlike false eyelashes and magnified by her round pink glasses.

Mabel had been shifting her feet, hoping to catch a glimpse of Grandma's books on the cart behind the counter. Now, she refocused on Thelma. "You knew him?" she repeated. "Did you have termites?"

"What?" Thelma drew back a bit.

"Like Ms. Katherine Ann. She hired him to exterminate her bugs."

"Oh!" Thelma giggled. "Goodness, no. I didn't even know the man was an exterminator. No, I knew him from right here. He attended the coin club that meets in the basement."

"Wow. That must've been a shock then."

Thelma leaned back and patted her chest. "Oh, a terrible shock. Of course, I only talked to him in passing over the years, but to think you see someone twice a month for a decade or so. And he's as alive as you and me. And then, he's dead. Not just dead — murdered."

She seemed to hyperventilate as she thought about it. "I never knew a murdered person before."

"I didn't either," Mabel said. "Not that I knew him, of course. But I never found a dead body at all before this."

"You know …" Thelma rested her bosom on the counter again and her head on one hand, seemingly oblivious to another patron hovering with a stack of books a few steps to Mabel's left. "I just keep asking myself, 'Why?' Why would anyone want to kill Carl Schuster?" She launched into a discourse on the general deterioration of society since she was a girl.

Mabel shifted her feet and slid an apologetic glance at the waiting patron who was now sighing audibly and looking pointedly at the clock. Finally, the young woman — who had a fussy toddler pulling at her shirt tail — dumped her books onto the counter with a crash. Thelma jumped.

"I'm so sorry, but I really need to get Scooter home. It's been a long day."

Thelma's brow creased, but she bit off whatever she'd been about to say. Quickly, she ran through the stack and handed the woman her charge slip. "Have a nice day," she said with a cheery wave for the squawking little boy. "Now, where were we?"

Lisa would be getting impatient, but maybe Thelma had something worthwhile to contribute. "You were wondering why Carl Schuster was murdered."

"That's right. But all I knew about him was Coin Club, and that could hardly have been involved. There are probably ten or fifteen members that come and go, but a few like Carl are here just about every month. Mostly men. Carl was one of the younger ones.

"They talked to me sometimes. It was all 'obverse this' and 'double-die that.' Meaningless gibber. You know …" She shifted her bosom and rested her chin in her other hand. "I used to collect coins. Every Christmas when I was still in school, my uncle used to give me those blue books you'd stick pennies in? I—"

Deciding rudeness was the only way she'd ever cut through the one-sided stream of conversation, Mabel jumped in. "Did you come up with any theories? Involving the coin club?"

Thelma startled. Maybe she'd forgotten Mabel was there. "Well, no …"

Mabel was just about to give up and ask for Grandma's books again, when Thelma started back up. "Except, I did wonder if it could be something like when we had that big theft back in—oh, I guess you wouldn't remember that. You weren't living here then. It was that old man who supposedly owned all those valuable coins … Jackson, was it? Of course, you wouldn't know, but—"

"Thelma." Randolph McKew, the head librarian, spoke quietly as he appeared from the office behind the desk.

At the rumble of his deep voice, both Thelma and Mabel startled.

"I need you to go shelve books now. Check if anyone's in the carrels and let them know we'll soon be closing."

Thelma showed no evidence of embarrassment at being caught gossiping. "Give my love to your grandma. Tell her I'll be stopping by one day soon."

A bit resentfully, Mabel gave Mr. McKew Grandma's request as, out of the corner of her eye, she watched Thelma go. After she'd wasted all that time, the librarian's appearance had come at exactly the wrong moment. Just when it looked like they were finally getting somewhere.

When she got back to the car, Lisa immediately started the engine. "I was beginning to wonder if I needed to come in and look back in the stacks for *your* body."

"I'm sorry." Mabel set Grandma's books on the back seat. "I got roped into a thing with Thelma Neuhaus." She waved a hand in response to Lisa's look of befuddlement. "An old friend of Grandma's. She never stops talking."

"Peach's Market next, then."

"Yeah ..." Mabel gazed out the window as Lisa wove through the streets and headed toward the outskirts of town. Teenagers lounged on the corner outside Murph's Record Mart, which had been there since the 1950s. Nowadays, Murph's nephew still sold vinyl, mostly used, out of the back, but magazines, comics, and snacks from the front of the store likely paid the bills. The peeling trim was in need of a paint job—something the present owner probably couldn't afford.

"Hey, Lisa. You've lived here for a while now. Do you remember a big coin theft? Some old guy's collection. I can't remember the name, but Thelma didn't seem too sure anyway. Maybe started with a J?"

Lisa slipped her a sidelong glance. "I don't think so. What's that got to do with anything?"

"Maybe nothing. Just Thelma mentioned Carl—the Bug Man—was a member of the coin club that meets at the library. She had some theory the murder might've had something to do with stolen coins. And she mentioned that one theft."

"Nope. I'd ask your grandma and her buddies."

The market was uncrowded. While Mabel selected a disgusting-looking tube of liver sausage, Lisa ran to the freezer section for Grandma's requested cherry-vanilla. In less than ten minutes, they were back on the road home.

Once again, Ms. Katherine Ann's Cadillac occupied the side driveway and a portion of the forsythia bushes. Laughter came through the open living room window. *Perfect.* Mabel would have access to the collective memory of all three old ladies.

Fireflies flitted across the grass, flashing their tiny green lanterns. When Mabel opened the back door, Barnacle launched himself at them, bouncing and jumping back and forth between her and Lisa.

"Mabel." Grandma's shout came from the living room. "Did you bring the ice cream?"

"Yes, I did. Hang on."

"Fetch us three bowls, would you, baby?"

"Sure thing."

Once again, the old friends were sitting together in the front room. Paper plates littered with pizza crust sat atop the back of the piano, out of Barnacle's reach. "Hello, girls." Miss Birdie greeted them. "Doesn't that ice cream look good on a warm evening?"

As Lisa passed the dishes around, Mabel decided to launch right into her questions. "I ran into Mrs. Neuhaus at the library this evening. She said to give you her love and that she'd be over to see you soon."

Grandma sighed. "She's a good-hearted soul."

Ms. Katherine Ann rolled her eyes despite a stern look from Miss Birdie.

"Hey, she told me something kind of interesting, but we got interrupted."

"That's a blessing," Ms. Katherine Ann muttered.

"I wondered if any of you ladies might know anything more about it. It was about the Bug Man."

"She could probably use their services." Ms. Katherine Ann looked up. "Thelma's no housekeeper."

"Katherine." Miss Birdie shook her head.

"You know it's true."

"Just go ahead and tell us, Mabel dear," Grandma said. "You were saying?"

"Just that, you know, she said the Bug Man — Carl Schuster — was a regular at the library coin club."

"The paper did say something about that." Miss Birdie tilted her head. "That he collected coins."

Lisa hadn't had a theory earlier. Now, suddenly she made a little squeak and poked Mabel in the ribs.

Mabel had no clue what that outburst was about. *What?* she mouthed, but Lisa just shook her head.

"Anyway," Mabel continued, "Mrs. Neuhaus mentioned something about a coin theft? She said an old man's collection was stolen."

"Here lately?" Ms. Katherine Ann shook her head. "I never heard anything about that, did you?" She looked back and forth from Miss Birdie to Grandma.

"Sure you did," Miss Birdie told her. "Not lately though. Remember Jubilee Johnson?"

"Whew." Grandma leaned forward. "I haven't thought about him in over twenty years."

"Probably closer to twenty-five since it happened," Miss Birdie said. She turned to Mabel. "You know the Johnson mansion, don't you, baby?"

Mabel thought hard. "The haunted house?"

"Don't be foolish, Mabel." Grandma frowned at Ms. Katherine Ann, who'd been nodding in agreement. "There's no such thing. But if you mean the abandoned house on Cherry Orchard Road, that's the one Birdie's talking about. Old Mr. Johnson had no family, and he let that place run down. It burned to a shell a couple years after he died, so it does look pretty creepy."

"Pretty creepy" didn't do the Johnson place justice. Only the stone wall along the road and the outer stonework of the old house still stood.

Fire hadn't yet gutted the interior when Mabel first saw it, during her childhood summer visits with Grandma. But even then, well over thirty years ago, wild vines and saplings had already grown up around the dark hulk of the house, choking out the former lawn and gardens. It looked like the tangle that had grown up around Snow White's coffin in the fairytale even then. And the neighborhood kids already said it was haunted, despite the fact old Mr. Johnson was still living in there somewhere.

Mabel had lost track of it, and old Mr. Johnson, once she'd grown up. "The coins belonged to the miser?"

"Mabel Josephine." Grandma tilted her head and arched her eyebrows warningly at the portrait of Jesus that hung above the TV. "You're too old to be talking like that. Mr. Johnson was just a lonely old man who was confused in his head when he got older. He was certainly not a miser."

"I'm sorry," Mabel mumbled. "I never knew him. That's just what the kids always said about him — that he had a ton of money hidden on the property but was too cheap to spend it."

Miss Birdie laughed — a soft ripple she hid behind her hand. "Oh, baby, those were just kids' stories. That poor man barely had two nickels to rub together. He lived on Meals-on-Wheels and canned beans. Our church ladies tried to lend a hand, but he was too proud to accept it. After he passed, God rest his soul, the county took the property for back taxes."

"The county still owns it?" Lisa asked.

Ms. Katherine Ann nodded. "First, they were going to put it up for auction, but then the house burned down."

"There was talk they were going to use the acreage for a park, but that never seemed to go anywhere." Grandma shifted to a more comfortable position.

Mabel frowned. "But he had a valuable coin collection, right? Doesn't that suggest he was richer than he let on?"

Miss Birdie shrugged. "Heard he inherited those coins from someone, and added onto the collection as he could, while he was still working."

"Did they ever recover what was stolen?" Mabel asked.

All three old ladies shook their heads. "Never did, that I heard," Miss Birdie said. "The old man was already pretty muddled up in his head by the time he got robbed, so he wasn't much help to the police."

"The coins never turned up on the market, I don't believe, and *I* still think the whole story was fishy somehow." Grandma folded her arms as if ready to challenge anybody who disagreed.

"Fishy how?" Mabel leaned against the doorframe, preparing for a long listen.

"Mr. Johnson was what you call a recluse. Kept to himself — only ever saw the Meals-On-Wheels driver once in a while, and his aide from the Agency on Aging, and they both said he didn't make much sense when he talked. Neither of them ever saw these coins he was making such a fuss about."

"What?" Lisa said. "You don't think they ever existed?"

"No proof they ever did, and that's for sure," Miss Birdie said.

"He just came walking into town one day — people thought they were seeing a ghost. All raggedy and scraggle-headed. Just wailing and carrying on about being robbed." Ms. Katherine Ann shook her head. "He thought somebody was living in his attic and sneaking downstairs at night, and all kinds of foolishness."

"Anyway," Grandma said, "the police did investigate, but never found the coins. And Mr. Johnson died soon after. That's the only coin robbery or anything like that I know of around here."

The other two women nodded agreement.

Super progress. A burned-down house, a confused old man who'd died years ago, and a "stolen" coin collection that likely as not had never existed. And even if it had, the theft had occurred so long ago that Carl Schuster had been a child when it happened.

As she and Lisa said their goodbyes, Mabel's glance rested on the old bookcase. Grandma had a whole shelf full of Perry Mason mystery novels, most of which Mabel had read on her visits, growing up. They had fueled her ambition to become a lawyer, a career she'd imagined would involve matching wits with killers and bringing them to justice. That daydream had certainly crashed and burned.

It was pretty clear her new aspiration to be a citizen detective was similarly doomed to failure. Mabel vowed to forget trying to solve a murder and concentrate instead on rescuing a little stray cat.

Chapter Sixteen

Mabel soon realized her vow to forget the Bug Man's murder had failed to take account of Lisa. As they drove through the quiet streets, Lisa thought out loud. "What if the Bug Man stole those coins? And somebody found out and came after them?"

Mabel shook her head. "If Grandma and her gang are right, the only coin theft in Medicine Spring history happened when Carl Schuster was a very little kid."

Lisa drove on in silence for a couple minutes, then hit her brakes in the middle of the block. "How about this? What if somebody from the coin club did it, and the Bug Man found out and he had to be silenced?"

Mabel was glad she'd been wearing a shoulder harness. She unbuckled her seatbelt and loosened it again, so she could breathe. "That still doesn't account for his being in that house, though, does it?"

Lisa drove on in silence for a moment. Mabel could almost hear the clicking of her brain, turning over the possibilities.

Despite herself, Mabel's brain was doing the same thing. Maybe, she thought, her story didn't have to end with failing to become the new female Perry Mason. "Oh, my gosh," she breathed. "I've got it. What if the owner of the house stole the coins, and when Schuster was there to exterminate, he discovered them? *What if they're still there?*"

Now it was Lisa who frowned. "Wouldn't they have taken them when they moved? Plus, there have been two whole families living in that house since the burglary happened. *If* it happened."

Mabel made a face. Lisa was right, of course. But her newly developing citizen-detective brain cells kept clicking away. "I just need to think some more. I've almost got it."

The streetlights had come on, but an almost tangible darkness enfolded the Gundersen house. Mabel hopped out. "Hang on a sec while I grab the key."

Mabel trotted up Pete's well-lit walk to retrieve the door key from under the glider cushions. When she turned back around, she muffled a shriek, realizing Lisa was directly behind her.

"What? I'm not going to stand in the shadows by myself, waiting for the murderer to return to the scene of the crime."

"Do they really do that?"

"Sometimes."

Mabel considered the dark bulk of the empty house, and its blank, curtainless windows. "But not, like, usually, right?"

"Nah. Just when they have unfinished business. Or if they want to gloat over their work."

Mabel swallowed. "What kind of unfinished business?"

"Oh, like maybe they got interrupted and didn't get what they came for the first time. Or maybe they think they might've left a clue they want to clean up."

The driveway was empty. So was the curb. If the murderer had returned to the scene of the crime, he'd have had to be on foot.

Mabel looked up. No lights at all in the house, that she could see. She scanned the dark mounds of the bushes. Nothing moved. Fireflies flickered over the yard, undisturbed.

When an SUV passed by, then turned into a nearby driveway, Mabel shook off her attack of nerves. She was letting Lisa's true-crime obsession get to her … probably because she knew tonight nobody was home next door.

"Come on. Let's get in there," she said. "Do you have your hardware to fix the trap?"

Lisa lifted the brown paper bag. "You have your bait?"

"Braunschweiger."

"Huh? What's that?"

"Liver sausage."

Lisa's lip curled.

"Cats and dogs can't resist it. The smell's going to attract her even if she's all the way outside."

"And probably every wild animal in a one-mile radius."

"Not unless they can climb up there and squeeze through a tiny opening in that broken window."

"Well, let's get this over with. I wish we'd come earlier. I hate the thought of messing around in there in the dark."

Mabel trained her flashlight beam on the lock and inserted the key. When they'd slipped inside, she aimed the light at the stairs. Her nose wrinkled. She hadn't really noticed the musty smell before that the house had acquired from standing empty in the summer heat and humidity.

Maybe Gundersens would air it out when they came. Thinking of them also brought her mind back to Koi. Mabel hoped they wouldn't take her. Marge already had more cats than she could take care of.

Lisa gave Mabel's back a little shove. "Wake up."

Mabel climbed the staircase, pointing the feeble beam at her feet. *Darn.* She should've taken a moment to check her batteries. They'd have to work fast.

As they reached the top of the stairs, she paused. Lisa rammed into her.

"What is it now?" Lisa muttered.

Uneasy, Mabel gestured toward the murder room, where she'd been setting the trap each night, and found herself whispering. "That's weird. It almost looks like there's a light on."

The faint glow washing over the door sill might have barely registered if the hall hadn't been dark as two AM in a coal mine. Lisa leaned around her for a look. "Just light from outside coming through the window."

Mabel couldn't have quite explained why, but she switched off her own failing flash. At another little shove from behind, she started tiptoeing toward the bedroom.

At the threshold, Mabel's mouth went dry, and she froze. The room was occupied.

A penlight rested on the floor, casting its beam at the opposite baseboard and sending up weird, elongated streaks of shadow. In the dim illumination, a figure knelt, back turned to the doorway.

It was only a silhouette, but Mabel recognized Jack Armbruster right away — or rather, Armbruster's son with the wild mop of dark hair. He seemed to be jabbing at something she couldn't see.

Her heart lurched in her chest, and she eased back a step, in hopes of making a silent exit.

Lisa shrieked. "Good grief, Mabel! Watch what you're doing."

The man whirled around and scrambled to his feet, shooting the intense stream of light directly into her eyes.

130

Mabel scrunched her lids shut and threw an arm up to block the beam.

Behind her, Lisa sucked in a breath and slowly released it. "Hey …"

The man loomed over Mabel, penlight in one hand and a pry bar clenched in the other.

Mabel's breath seemed stuck in her throat. Did he recognize her from the day she discovered the Bug Man's body? From the path by the pond? She drew in shallow gulps of air. *Natural. Be natural.* "Oh, hi." She waved her tube of liverwurst at him. "Hey, I wonder … Could you possibly lower that? You're blinding me."

For a miracle, he did bring the flashlight down a few inches. Mabel wondered if the angle was making her look like the Bride of Frankenstein. Armbruster was a good ten or fifteen years younger than she was, but the upward light beam was doing him no favors either, creating harsh valleys at the side of his mouth and making his eyes glitter in cave-like sockets.

She pointed at the trap. "We're just here for the cat. The stray that hangs around here? The guy next door has been taking care of the place, and he doesn't want it to get shut up inside when he fixes the broken window on this floor. We've been trying for a few days, but it keeps stealing the bait, and yesterday, it didn't even bother it at all. I think it was getting tired of chicken, so I went and bought some liverwurst."

She brandished the wobbling plastic-cased tube again, but Armbruster's wary expression never changed.

Mabel nearly giggled, a nervous habit she'd thought she'd outgrown her sophomore year in high school. "Anyway, I figured no cat could resist the aroma of good old liver sausage. That's funny, isn't it? It's not very popular with people, but cats seem to love it.

"So anyway," she repeated, "we just came by to set the trap again. And of course, try to fix the trap a little bit better. So it's more sensitive?" Mabel gestured behind her for Lisa to display her bag from the hardware.

But Lisa wasn't there.

Mabel changed her gesture to a casual, leisurely stretch. Briefly, she considered removing Lisa from her Christmas list.

"Do you know anything at all about traps?" She knew she was babbling but couldn't seem to stop herself. "Have you noticed a little cat around here? She's mostly black with a bit of gold. Very fluffy. The last time I saw her, she had a limp."

Mabel opened her mouth to continue her monologue, but the man raised one hand like a traffic cop. "Sorry, no. I haven't seen a cat around here. And I don't know a thing about traps. Just checking out the old place, you know? I grew up here, years ago. This used to be my bedroom."

Mabel's eyes flicked toward the baseboard where he'd been kneeling, but shadows cloaked it now.

He laughed briefly as if he'd caught her glance. "Just seeing if I could find where I carved my initials when I was a kid. Boy, was my mom mad."

Mabel managed a weak laugh. Her eyes shifted toward the trap sitting on the floor in front of the closet.

Armbruster's flashlight swept that direction. As it did, the beam revealed a gaping hole in the floor, where the heat register had been pulled up. Mabel also caught a passing glint of gold at the bottom of the baseboard. Was it just one of those butterscotch wrappers? Odd that it was right where Armbruster had been working.

"Police must've pulled that up," he said. "Just lucky I didn't put my foot there in the dark—I could've broken my neck."

"Wow, that's for sure." Mabel backed up a step. She'd been here every day for a week now. That grate had still been in place after the police had cleared the house.

"I could've stepped in it myself." She motioned toward the closet beyond. "I was just thinking about setting the trap, but it needs to be adjusted, and my friend has the hardware. I better go see where she got to. I can come back another time."

"I know you." He frowned. "You were here the day they found that body in here."

Mabel waved the liverwurst airily. "Oh, were you here too? Looked like half the neighborhood turned out."

His eyes narrowed.

"Awful, wasn't it? Poor man. Anyway, like I say, I should get going. Nice to meet you." She realized she was babbling again, but her mind wasn't on her words. It was on that crowbar.

And wondering what on earth he was doing here.

Had Armbruster killed the Bug Man?

Suddenly, a loud clunk downstairs shook the floor.

Mabel's overstretched nerves snapped. She threw the liverwurst at Armbruster's face, but her aim went wild, as usual. The sausage struck his penlight, knocking it to the floor, and immediately the light went out.

She spun around and scrambled for the hallway. *Aarrgghh* … If she was going to miss his face, why hadn't she knocked the pry bar out of his hand?

As Mabel dove for the open doorway, a small black mass flew between her feet. She staggered, turning partway back toward the murder room. The faint light from the streetlamp streaming through the bedroom window across the hall illuminated the little cat as she launched herself into the gaping hole in the floor.

Mabel tried to right herself but stumbled over the door threshold. Feeling herself going down, she made a desperate grab for the doorframe.

Just as her fingers brushed it, Armbruster plowed into her from behind.

Mabel crashed hard on her left hip with him on top of her. She threw both arms up in front of her face and flailed at him, trying to fend off the pry bar he was still clutching. She struggled to get to her feet.

But suddenly, she heard the clunk of the pry bar hitting the floor. Armbruster's weight lifted off, and he was running for the stairs.

Mabel rose to her hands and knees, panting and staring after him into the dim hallway. She wasn't dead. That was something to be thankful for, once she was able to wrap her head around whatever had just happened.

Armbruster's feet crashed and stumbled down the staircase. It sounded as if he was taking two or three steps at a time.

Mabel straightened and steadied herself on the banister. Cautiously, she crept forward, peering over the railing as she went. The outside lights revealed the curve of the banister as it joined the newel post at the bottom.

Armbruster skidded and fell hard as he missed the final step, scrambled to his feet, and lurched toward the back door.

Mabel inched down the stairs. Where was Lisa?

A commotion came from the kitchen area at the rear of the house. Torn, Mabel looked toward the front door and freedom, then at the back hall. Lisa might be in danger.

Chewing the inside of her lip, she headed for the kitchen.

She crept forward, one hand trailing along the wall, till she could see the room. Armbruster stood facing the back door, hunched shoulders heaving, and with both arms in the air.

"Who's back there?" a harsh male voice snapped.

"It's me — Mabel. Um … don't shoot."

Chapter Seventeen

Pete stood silhouetted in the outside doorway of the kitchen, shotgun in hand. "Did this scumbag hurt you, little girl?"

"No. I'm okay."

"Best step outta the line of fire, Mabel. You go on out the front. I got an itchy trigger finger and if this guy moves an eyelash, my peacemaker's liable to go off."

"Come on, man! You know me," Armbruster whined with sweat in his voice. "I'm your old neighbor. You remember—Danny Armbruster."

"I sure as heck remember you don't live in this house anymore. Mabel, if you got a phone, you go on and call the police. We're gonna sort this out right here and now."

Mabel scuttled backward into the safety of the darkened hallway. Surely, Pete wouldn't actually shoot, would he?

She rocketed toward the front door, fumbling with her phone.

"911. What's your emergency?"

Mabel stared at the red and blue lights strobing across the glass panels on either side of the door. "Never mind. The police are already here."

Lisa stood at the curb, chattering at two policemen, arms waving madly as she gestured at the house. Mabel couldn't make out a word she said, but Lisa beckoned her. A standard cruiser sat parked nose to nose with a police SUV.

As she approached, a snarling German shepherd in the back of the SUV lunged at the windows. Mabel jumped.

One of the officers held up a hand in front of Lisa's face, then turned to Mabel. "Is the suspect still inside?"

"Yes. By the back door."

"Armed?"

"I ... I don't think so. But the neighbor is. He's holding a gun on him right now."

The cop's eyes narrowed.

"The neighbor's been taking care of the place for the owners since they left," Lisa said.

The officer reached back inside the car for a megaphone. "Don't go anywhere."

As the police walked off toward the house, Mabel breathed a sigh of relief to watch the agitated police dog go with them. "Thanks for calling the cops."

Lisa's eyes were huge. "What happened in there? Did he hurt you?"

Mabel shook her head. "I'm honestly not sure *what* happened. I thought he was coming at me with that pry bar, but then, we both just sort of crashed when he ran into me, and he dropped it anyway. Then he ran for the doors, and Pete was there with his gun."

"What was he up to?"

"I don't know, but he seemed to be trying to get under the baseboard. And part of the floor was up too."

"Do you think ...?"

"That he killed the Bug Man? Maybe. Seems like too much for coincidence that he keeps popping up— especially there. No idea why, though."

"It must have something to do with whatever he was looking for."

Mabel nodded, looking back toward the house. A couple neighbors had come out onto their porches but seemed hesitant to step into the open. "I hope they let me back inside. The cat was there. And I left my liverwurst."

The amplified voice of the cop with the megaphone came from the back. "Police. Put down your weapon."

"I guess we need to wait. Not that I'd leave before I find out what was going on in there anyway," Mabel said.

About twenty minutes elapsed before Armbruster, wearing cuffs, walked around the front corner, followed by the police. They put him in the back of the cruiser, and the officer drove away while the second officer loaded the dog into the SUV.

The K-9 officer sighed and pointed at Mabel. "Let's get a statement from you. McAllister says every time he turns around, you've been showing up all over this case."

Mabel sputtered, prepared to defend herself, but he cut her off. "Just the facts."

As succinctly as possible, Mabel ran through why she'd been inside the house, and what had happened. Finally, they seemed to have exhausted her entire store of knowledge, which was limited.

The officer closed his notepad. "Can you make it to the station tomorrow sometime to sign this?"

Mabel nodded. "Um ..." She darted a look toward the second-floor windows. "I'm wondering if I might be allowed to go up and try to either grab the cat or set my trap?"

"I guess you can come ahead. Mr. Dombroski ran back to his place to call the homeowner. But by now he's probably waiting to go up and check for damage. We took Armbruster in for questioning. At this point, it just looks like trespass. Apparently, he used to live here. You say he didn't try to hurt you. The only reason we're drilling down a bit is that body that turned up here. And you say he was prying at the floor and baseboard. Doesn't smell right."

"Thanks." Mabel started toward the house with Lisa following.

"Hey," the cop called after them.

She turned back.

"Hold on. I'm headed up too. We warned Mr. Dombroski about firearm safety, but he might be a little nervous right now."

"Good point!" Mabel hung back and let the cop go first.

"Yo," the officer called as they approached the rear of the house.

"Yo," Pete called back.

"Old Phil's madder than a hornet about the Armbruster kid breaking in," Pete said, as they came face to face. "They never did control that kid, and now look at him."

Lisa opened her mouth, and Mabel stepped on her foot. A lecture wouldn't be helpful right now.

"Well, let's go up and take a look." The officer waved Pete ahead.

The pry bar still lay across the doorway. Pete stepped over it, as did the police officer.

Lisa shone her flashlight around the room, and the beam danced with Pete's and the cop's lights. The cop froze his beam on the battered tube of liverwurst. "What's this?"

"Oh, that's mine." Mabel picked it up. "It's my cat bait."

The cop brightened. "I love braunschweiger."

"Me too." Pete shone his light on the sausage. "The wife won't have it in the house. She says it's sick."

The cop shook his head. "You use mayo with it?"

"You gotta be kidding." Pete shook his head. "Mustard. You gotta have mustard and a big ol' slice of onion on there."

"Swiss?"

"Nah, we're mostly German."

"I was talking cheese. Man, I haven't seen this stuff in ages."

"Is it okay if I just go ahead and set my trap?" Mabel rolled her eyes. "You guys can split the leftovers if you want."

"Go ahead." The cop shone his light at the baseboard. "This where he was working?"

"Yeah." Mabel squinted. "What *is* that?"

Pete and the police officer squeezed past her. "It looks like the edge of a gold coin or some kind of token," Pete said.

Behind them, Lisa made a muffled squeak. Pete and the policeman turned.

She clamped a hand over her mouth.

"What?" the cop asked. "You okay?"

"Nothing."

The heavy-duty flash beam traveled around the empty room. It stopped over the hole in the floor. A cast-iron grating lay beside the opening.

"Old heat register," Pete said. "My grandparents had these on their second floor. I could lay on my stomach and look down at my grandma cooking oatmeal on the woodstove."

Mabel peered into the hole. "Huh. Just another floor below this one. Like a crawlspace."

"That's a dropped ceiling." Pete pointed upward. "All the ceilings in this place used to be way high. That's how they used to build them. Then, when people got smart and figured out they were wasting heat, they lowered them all. You're looking down at the kitchen ceiling."

"Maybe he hid something in there, if he used to live here," Mabel suggested.

Lisa crowded close and stared down at the crawlspace. "And he came back for it, and ran into the Bug Man."

"And they fought over it." Mabel's heart started to pound as a picture started to emerge in her head. "The Bug Man ends up dead."

"Coins!" She and Lisa yelled at the same time.

"Wait a minute." The cop was scowling now. "You two are getting … what do you call it? Behind your skis. What coins?" He pointed toward the baseboard. "There's maybe a coin over there if we dig it out and get a better look. You know something about that?"

"It's 'over your skis' — I mean the saying is. I don't mean you are. I'll try to slow down." Mabel caught her breath. "Can we look at that coin?"

"Not right now — might turn out it's evidence. Leave it be."

"Armbruster was only a kid when he left here," Pete said. "He was in trouble a lot, but nothing serious. Pranks and stuff."

"They knew each other," Lisa said.

"They graduated together, at least." Mabel handed Lisa the liverwurst.

Lisa curled her lip.

"Let me just look. I won't touch anything." Mabel stretched out on her stomach and shone her light around the crawlspace.

The beam caught a pair of glowing green eyes a few feet off. The little cat sat, calmly staring back at Mabel. Coins, dull with dust or tarnish, lay scattered around her.

Chapter Eighteen

Lisa answered her phone next morning just as Mabel was about to give up. "I'm baking blueberry-lemon bread. You want to come over and help me eat it?"

"I'd love to. I've got all kind of news to trade you."

"Oohh … You don't need to stay with your grandma?"

"Nope. Her Saturday Bible study is meeting at the house this morning."

Lisa's tiny one-bedroom apartment perched above Barb's Gift & Candle Nook on Main Street, next door to The Coffee Cup diner. Mabel parked in one of the diagonal spots a few doors down and climbed the narrow stairs to the second floor.

The sunny aroma of lemons and subtle tang of blueberries wafted from under the apartment door. Mabel had scarcely raised her hand to knock when Lisa called, "It's open."

"I know you heard me coming, but I could've been an ax murderer."

"I saw you park, duh. Is that what I think it is?"

Mabel set the cat carrier on the floor by Lisa's rain boots and umbrella stand. "Whom. And yup!"

"Are you going to let her out to explore?"

Mabel stared. "You're kidding, right? I spent days trying to catch this thing, and I don't want her escaping into your ductwork."

"I don't have ductwork."

"It's a figure of speech. I don't want her peeing on your floor either."

"Good point." Lisa knelt on the floor and peered inside the crate. "Well, hi, there, little girl."

Koi let out a long, mournful meow.

"Lemon-blueberry bread?"

"Cooling on the table. Just help yourself."

Mabel washed her hands at the sink and then flopped into a chair. Lisa's apartment was so cute and tiny ... like she was. Everything was white and clean — cabinets, stove and fridge, the small round table with its red legs and matching white chairs with red cushions. Handmade white curtains printed with red cherries hung at the windows — two looking down on Main Street and the side window looking out at the red-brick side of the hardware's second floor.

She took a plate from the stack in the center and cut two fat slices to put on it.

Lisa got up and filled the tea kettle. "Want some breakfast tea?"

Mabel's mouth was jammed with lemon-blueberry bread, but she nodded.

As soon as she'd swallowed, she exclaimed, "Guess what."

Her exclamation collided with Lisa's "Tell me your news before I explode. Is it about the cat?"

"No. I mean that too, but Danny Armbruster confessed. He murdered the Bug Man."

Lisa plopped into a chair. "Omigosh. Tell me everything."

Mabel hurried to chew a big bite of the blueberry bread while she cut another slice. "I missed breakfast," she apologized.

"Go ahead. You can talk with your mouth full. I've known you since you were five."

"What's that supposed to mean?"

"Nothing. Just no need to be polite. Talk, woman."

"This bread's really good. Thanks, Lis."

"Thanks, and you're welcome. How did you find out? How did he do it? Why did he kill him?"

"Well ..." Mabel settled in to tell her story. She loved to take her time with big news like this and refused to be rushed. "You know I had to go in to sign my statement for the police this morning. I wanted to check the cat trap first, but I was running late."

"So you went right to the police station first, and they said ...?"

Mabel sighed. "Anyway, Aunt Officer Debbie was working the front desk."

"Aww, I haven't seen her in years. Remember when she used to guard the crosswalk during Firemen's Carnival?"

"Yeah. She must be in her seventies now. She said she fills in at the desk when people are off. She told me Danny confessed last night. Seems like he killed the Bug Man kind of spontaneously."

"So not murder one."

"Right ... if you believe him. No premeditation. Anyway, they knew each other in high school, but weren't friends or anything. But they ran into each other at the last class reunion and started talking."

A howl emanated from the carrier.

"She's sad." Lisa looked toward the gloomy little face pressed against the bars, obviously weakening. "C'mon. I'm not allowed pets up here, but I guess it wouldn't hurt to let her out to explore a little bit. I can't stand seeing her like this."

"No." Mabel clamped a hand on Lisa's wrist before she could get up. "Maybe you're forgetting how long it took me to capture her in the first place?"

"Where could she go in a one-bedroom apartment?"

"I don't care to find out."

Lisa scooted over to slip Koi a bit of her blueberry bread. "I don't think she wants it."

"No kidding. She wants out."

"I hope you can tame her." Lisa slipped into her chair with a wistful look back.

"She'll be fine, once she knows I'm her friend." *I hope.*

"Go on." Lisa poured more tea, which Mabel doctored with a generous spoonful of sugar and a slug of milk.

"So you remember the coins that were stolen from that rich old man, years ago? Both Danny and the Bug Man were real little kids when that happened. And Danny's father was the old man's overnight aide.

"Anyway, at some point, Danny found a stash of coins his dad had squirreled away at home. At that stage of his childhood, Danny was fascinated with a charity coin collecting machine at the local pizza place. You know the wishing well things where you drop your coin in an opening and it spins around a spiral tube and down through a hole and into a barrel?"

"Sure. I still love those things. Where they have one when I take the kids on a field trip, I always drop a quarter in too when the kids are done."

"So I guess he decided to play wishing well at home and drop coins into the heating grate in his bedroom floor."

Lisa laughed. "Sounds typical."

Koi yowled again, as if she wanted to chime in too.

"Do you mind if I stick her in your bathroom for a while?"

"Go ahead. She's making me feel bad."

A moment later, Mabel returned and cut another chunk of blueberry bread. "At least, she's muffled a bit now."

"WHAT?" Lisa held a hand up to her ear.

"Funny." All the same, Mabel raised her voice. "I don't know how many coins he dropped in there, but apparently, he went back to his dad's cache more than once and helped himself to another one each time."

"I presume those were the stolen coins," Lisa said. "And Danny's dad—the filthy, elder-abusing crook—never noticed they were disappearing from his hoard?"

"I don't know. Aunt Officer Debbie never said. I'm guessing not. He probably just pilfered one or two when he could and stashed them all for later. I doubt he knew the first thing about what they were or which were more valuable than others. If he did know, he'd have had a fit or searched or something, right?"

"I'd think so."

"After a while, Danny lost interest in the coin game, and years later, the family moved away."

"Leaving the coins under the floor." Lisa shook her head. "And Danny never figured out what they were?"

Mabel shook her head. "He barely remembered a game he used to play when he was like three years old."

"Nobody suspected his dad of the theft?"

"He might've been questioned, but he had a clean record and was bonded by the company he worked for. The police had stronger leads at the time, but eventually, the whole thing died down. It's a shame he got away with it."

149

"Won't the cops be knocking on his door again, now that this is all coming out?"

Mabel shook her head. "The statute of limitations ran long ago. I hope those coins brought him nothing but misery. They sure ruined his son's life. And ended someone else's."

"So the Bug Man comes into the picture how?"

"The class reunion. Danny and Bug Man strike up a conversation, and Bug Man's boring him, droning on about his coin collection. Danny mentions his dad had some old coins, but probably nothing valuable. He laughs and adds, 'At least, I hope not—I used to play with them. Lost more than a few.' Of course, the Bug Man's antennas go up."

"Yuk, yuk."

"He says, 'What did they look like? Do you remember?' Danny describes one that looked kind of like a beat-up subway token. Bug Man says, 'That really might be worth something.'"

Lisa let out a little squeal and gave a mock shiver of excitement.

"Danny laughs and says, 'No way.' But when Schuster shows him a couple pictures on his phone, Danny nearly chokes. Some of those dingy slugs of metal are worth a ton of money. And he remembers the last time he saw a coin that looked almost like one of the pictures disappearing into a hole in his bedroom floor."

Mabel looked toward the bathroom door. "Maybe I should check on her. She's being too quiet."

"In a minute. Finish your story while I fix you a sandwich."

"Are you trying to keep me from eating all the blueberry bread?"

"I just want to hear why Danny killed the Bug Man. But maybe."

"Okay. What kind of sandwich?"

"I've got some leftover sloppy joe filling."

"Yum. Chips?"

"Yeah. Keep talking."

"Well, Danny pokes around a bit, and finds out his old house is now empty, at least temporarily."

Lisa paused her sandwich prep, rubber scraper in hand. "And meanwhile, the Bug Man can't stop thinking about the possibility the coins might still be in the house."

"Exactly."

"Now, did the Bug Man realize these were the actual coins from the robbery?"

Mabel shrugged. "I'm guessing so. Danny says he remembered enough to describe a few details about them to him. And according to Thelma at the library, Carl not only knew all about the original theft from old Mr. Johnson, he was kind of obsessed with it. The newspaper articles from back then even mention specific coins that disappeared and were never recovered."

The smell of warming sloppy joe filling wafted from the microwave. "Is that about ready?"

Lisa laughed. "Yeah. Hold on."

A scratching sound came from the bathroom, followed by a small meow.

"Oh, no," Lisa muttered. She and Mabel exchanged a startled look.

"No way. She couldn't have gotten out of that carrier." Mabel got up and crept closer to the bathroom door, only to see a small black paw reach out through the crack underneath.

Chapter Nineteen

Now what?" Lisa hovered over Mabel's shoulder. "Lunch is ready, by the way."

"Well …" Mabel considered. "I don't have a lot of options. We have to open that door eventually."

Lisa grimaced.

The scratching resumed.

"Mabel!" Lisa wailed. "She's going to ruin that door. If I lose my security deposit, I am not going to be a pleased puppy."

"Okay. Wait a sec. Do you have something like a spare pillowcase?"

"Exactly what do you have in mind?"

"I'm going to crack the door, and the instant she tries to run out, we'll pop the pillowcase over her like a bag."

"It'll never work." Lisa didn't budge.

"Do you have a better idea?"

"Well, no, but …"

"It's worth a try, anyway. If we leave her in there, she'll just keep scratching."

"All right, but I don't like this. She's pretty small. Like you said, if she escapes in here, we might not be able to catch her."

"Just get the pillowcase, okay? Or a laundry bag."

Lisa heaved a huge sigh but scurried off toward the bedroom.

A moment later, she reemerged with a pink-and-green-striped pillowcase.

"Thanks. When I say, 'go,' you ease the door open a crack, and I'm going to catch her in this."

"I'm really nervous about this."

"It'll be fine. Just ease it open very slowly. As soon as I get an idea where she's going to dart, I'll be ready." Secretly, Mabel felt anything but confident she could catch the tiny daredevil, but they had to try something before Koi damaged the door. She couldn't stay in there forever anyway.

She positioned herself on her knees with the pillowcase open. "Go!"

A bit shaky, Lisa cracked the door. The little cat squeezed her head through the opening. Then, just as quickly, the fuzzy head withdrew and reappeared as Koi flew over top Mabel's head as if shot from a cannon.

Lisa screamed.

Mabel scrambled to her feet, still clutching the pillowcase.

Either crying or laughing—perhaps both—Lisa pointed at the table, where Koi was efficiently gulping down sloppy joe, straight from the serving bowl. "Oh, nooo!" Mabel gasped.

"She was hungry." Lisa shrugged. "I guess we don't get lunch."

"That's probably horrible for her ... but she seems to like it."

"At least, she isn't running away. Do you think we could get her to trade up for a can of tuna?"

"Maybe. Or I guess we could just try dropping a laundry basket over her." Mabel studied the cat. "I don't want to scare her again."

"Poor thing. I can see her hipbones."

"I know. But at least her leg seems to be pretty well healed."

"Well, I'm going to try to feed her some canned tuna or chicken," Lisa announced. "If you try trapping her and miss, you'll probably scare her into hiding again."

"You're right. Just take it slow."

Surprisingly, the moment Lisa began opening the tuna can, Koi looked up from the sloppy joe bowl, her small muzzle ringed with red sauce. She meowed silently before leaping to the floor and padding over to where Lisa stood.

"Pretty girl," Lisa cooed. "You're a hungry kitty, aren't you?"

Koi sprang gracefully to the countertop. "Oh, baby. I'm going to have to sanitize everything in this place till you get done."

Mabel stared. "She's like a different cat. I can't believe how calm she is, especially after being trapped overnight."

Lisa reached out a tentative hand to stroke Koi's head but put it back down when the cat startled. "Still skittish."

"She didn't run, though. Maybe if we just quietly go about our business, she'll calm down enough for me to get her back in the carrier later."

Lisa studied the wreckage of their lunch. "Guess I'll dump that and clean off the table."

"I can't believe she's still eating." Mabel cast a fond eye on the skinny feline.

"I wish I could get a cat," Lisa said.

"Maybe if you offer to pay a pet deposit. That's what my building does."

"Well ..." Lisa closed the garbage can lid where she'd just dumped the ruined bowlful of lunch and handed Mabel a sanitizing wipe for the table. "What now?"

"You want to just order up from The Coffee Cup, and I can finish my story?"

"Sounds good."

***

By the time lunch had arrived and been consumed, Koi had filled her tummy and relaxed enough to fall asleep under a throw pillow on the couch. Feeling like a traitor, Mabel grabbed and stuffed her back in the carrier, then secured the latch with a bungee cord Lisa produced from her junk drawer, in hopes the extra fastener would keep the cat locked down till she got her home to Grandma's.

She finished telling Lisa her story but headed home soon thereafter. Grandma was waiting impatiently, along with Miss Birdie and Ms. Katherine Ann, who'd stayed behind after the Bible study meeting.

After much oohing and aahing from the old ladies over the unhappy little face in the carrier, Mabel carted her upstairs to the spare bedroom Grandma designated as "Koi's room." "I'll be right back," she promised the ladies, "and tell you all about it."

As she climbed the steps with her pitifully yowling cargo, Barnacle danced around her feet, sniffing and whining. "You're going to have to be a good big brother, okay? This is a very small girl, and she doesn't know you're a friend yet."

After settling Koi the best she could with a makeshift litter box and dishes of tuna and water, Mabel opened the carrier door and watched the cat take her first cautious step outside. She sniffed the air and seemed wary, as if ready to dart back inside at any moment.

"You poor baby." Mabel watched with a sympathetic eye. "You're safe now. You'll always have enough to eat, and I promise Barnacle won't be allowed in your room. When you're ready to check out the rest of the house, it'll be up to you, okay?"

Koi looked up at her and made a silent meow that seemed to indicate she understood and accepted the arrangement. Mabel slipped back into the hallway and headed downstairs, following the aroma of coffee mixed with a fruity fragrance.

"We just heated you up a nice piece of cherry pie," Ms. Katherine Ann told Mabel, shoving a plate at her.

"You want some coffee, baby?" Miss Birdie, her wiry figure loosely draped in a shirtwaist printed with tiny violets, held up the pot in one hand and a mug in the other.

"Thanks so much. Sure, I'd love some." Mabel felt she could get used to living here forever with three grandmotherly ladies to hover over her.

Grandma cleared a corner of the card table for her to put her plate down, and Miss Birdie set the coffee next to it. Creamer and sugar still occupied the center of the table, obviously left from the meeting.

"Thelma brought over the pie," Grandma said. "She has a gift."

Mabel had to agree. She closed her eyes and savored flaky, sugared crust and smooth, tart-but-sweet cherry filling.

Miss Birdie gently cleared her throat. "We've just been on pins and needles ever since we heard you captured the killer. But please take your time and enjoy your pie. We don't want to rush you."

"Why do you think they say 'pins and needles' anyway?" Miss Katherine Ann stretched and rearranged her bottom on the couch. "I can't even picture such a thing."

Mabel opened her mouth, had nothing to say about pins and needles, and decided to have another bite of pie. She held up one finger to ask her audience to hold on.

"For goodness' sake, Katherine." Grandma pointed at the rhinestone-encrusted cellphone cover protruding from a rhinestone-encrusted tote bag sitting at the end of the couch. "Look it up on your computer phone. Let Mabel finish her pie, so she can tell us about the murder."

"Just a sec. I'm almost done."

After doctoring her coffee with a generous shot of creamer and several spoonsful of sugar, she took a couple palate-cleansing sips. "Ah, that was good. Okay. Here we go ..."

Once again, Mabel started her tale with the long-ago coin theft.

"See," Grandma told Ms. Katherine Ann. "I knew it was about those coins—not flea treatment."

Ms. Katherine Ann waved a hand. "Hold on. She didn't tell us the whole story yet. There's bound to be fleas in it somewhere."

Mabel waited till the flea diversion had died down and then resumed her tale. "Apparently, Danny and Carl converged on the house at the same time." Mabel paused in her narrative to consider whether people could converge at different times and decided they could not. "They converged. Both of them were after the coins, and they ended up in a tussle. Danny insists he only attacked the Bug Man in self-defense, and that his death was an accident."

Miss Birdie gave a genteel snort. "They always say that."

"Well," Grandma said, "I guess there weren't any witnesses to say one way or another."

"Except maybe Koi." Mabel smiled.

"What about that bug van?" Ms. Katherine Ann asked. "I suppose Armbruster ditched it too?"

"He did." That, to Mabel, was nearly as chilling as the murder. "He took it down the access road in the middle of the night, jammed the accelerator, and sent it into the pond." *Right behind this house while Grandma was sleeping.*

"Quite a coincidence, your running into him back there, baby. It makes my blood run cold." Miss Birdie shivered.

"I wasn't in any danger," Mabel told Miss Birdie … and herself. "I had Barnacle."

"Why on earth did he go back there again?" Grandma asked. "Did he say?"

"It was the drought. He knew the water level in the pond had to be dropping, and he couldn't rest till he knew whether the van was still submerged."

"You think the Bug Man was gonna keep the coins if he found them?" Miss Birdie asked.

Mabel shrugged. "He's gone, so I guess we'll never know for sure. I'd like to think his motives were noble, but …"

"He was definitely a crook." Ms. Katherine Ann folded her arms.

"Well … his partner seemed to think so. Or wanted people to suspect Carl of those break-ins anyway, and not him. And Carl did have a copy of the house key he shouldn't have had. The cops will definitely be looking into that too."

"Oh, that's how he got in then." Grandma shifted in her chair as if the hip was bothering her.

"Yeah, they found it on him." Mabel frowned. "Do you need a pain pill?"

"No, baby, I'm good. I don't want to get hooked. This right now's no worse than my regular arthritis."

"But how did the other guy get in?" Miss Birdie asked. "The way you did?"

"No. He said he squeezed in through a tiny cellar window. He used to sneak in and out that way when he was a teenager. Knew how to pop it, and he was still skinny enough to go through."

"Did he manage to get any of the coins?" Grandma asked. "Since that's what he was there for — and killed the Bug Man over."

"He said no. He said after he realized he'd killed Carl, he freaked out and ran. He was afraid at first to go back. But he figured by now, things had finally died down enough.

"So yesterday he planned another quick stop at the house to try to snatch what he could before leaving town and heading home. I just blundered in at the wrong moment."

"Or the right moment." Miss Birdie patted Mabel's hand. "We're very proud of you, baby. Aren't we, girls?"

Mabel started to say she hadn't done anything special when a soft meow interrupted her.

The little tortoiseshell cat stood in the hall doorway, rubbing her fur against the frame.

"Now how did you get out again?" Mabel didn't know whether to be exasperated or proud of her kitten.

Barnacle popped up next to Koi, grinning as if he knew the secret. Apparently, they'd bonded — and possibly collaborated — while Mabel had been talking.

"Barnacle adores kitties," Grandma said comfortably. "He loved my old Ruthie, God rest her soul. Those two were always up to something."

Mabel studied the animal duo. It might've been a tic, but Barnacle certainly seemed to wink at her. She hoped they'd use their combined powers for good.

Author Note

Mabel & the Cat's Meow, a solo project of Susan Kimmel Wright, is a prequel to *Mabel Gets the Ax,* Book One in the *Mysteries of Medicine Spring* cozy mystery series from Mountain Brook INK Fiction.

I hope you'll want to follow Mabel & Koi's continuing adventures with Barnacle, Lisa, and the other residents of Medicine Spring.

Please visit me at my website, susankimmelwright.com, where you can also subscribe to my newsletter, the *Medicine Spring Bulletin* for news, fun, and giveaways.

Thanks so much for reading!

Made in the USA
Middletown, DE
15 June 2021